"I have read Marie Sheppard Willi of the Handicapped with enormous ... ... as if I were sitting at her feet, listening to her tales—not wanting them to end and, when they did, begging for more. Marie verbally paints, in the most delicate hues, people we have all met: the downhearted and downtrodden, the arrogant and manipulative, the mysterious and the simple. She is irreverent and cynical but never condescending or hurtful as she uncovers the handicaps in each of them, and in each of us. . . . Her book rings with joy and compassion." —Susan Hartman, Licensed Psychologist, Founder and Executive Director of CONNECT/US-Russia

---

"I am a 15-year veteran of the clinical social work profession, and I know that one of the most important tools I bring to my work is humor. Ms. Williams' stories are about knowing people and caring about them, and how caring and laughing go hand in hand. As I read them, laughter and a sense of our common humanity were my constant companions. I strongly recommend these stories to all who are in the helping professions."
—Ann J. Brown, LICSW

"These tales are such a breath of fresh air! Finally, someone has taken the time and daring to show that our 'clients' and/or 'patients' are just (!) human beings, not diagnoses, problems to be dealt with, crises to handle or issues to solve. . . . I am glad to see that Ms. Williams has been able to provide us an atlas to find our way back." —Ruthann Swanson, LICSW, Supervisor, Social Work Service, US Dept. Of Veteran Affairs

THE WORLDWIDE CHURCH
OF THE HANDICAPPED

THE WORLDWIDE CHURCH OF THE
HANDICAPPED
OF THE
and other stories by

Marie Sheppard Williams

 COFFEE HOUSE PRESS :: MINNEAPOLIS

The author wishes to thank the editors of The American Voice, where the follow-
ing stories appeared in somewhat different form: "The Sun, The Rain," "Wilma
Bremer's Funeral," and "The Book of Dreams." "The Sun, the Rain" was reprint-
ed in The Pushcart Prize XVIII; and "Wilma Bremer's Funeral" in The Pushcart
Prize XX. "Horghay-Loo-Ees-Bor-G-Hais" first appeared in The Alaska Quarterly
Review. "The Night Class" was published in Hurricane Alice in a cut version.

Coffee House Press is supported, in part, by a grant provided by the Minnesota
State Arts Board, through an appropriation by the Minnesota State Legislature,
and by a grant from the National Endowment for the Arts, a federal agency.
Additional support has been provided by the Lila Wallace-Reader's Digest Fund;
The McKnight Foundation; Lannan Foundation; Jerome Foundation; Target
Stores, Dayton's, and Mervyn's by the Dayton Hudson Foundation; General Mills
Foundation; St. Paul Companies; Honeywell Foundation; Star Tribune/Cowles
Media Company; Beverly J. and John A. Rollwagen Fund of The Minneapolis
Foundation; Prudential Foundation; and The Andrew W. Mellon Foundation.

Coffee House Press books are available to the trade through our primary distribu-
tor, Consortium Book Sales & Distribution, 1045 Westgate Drive, Saint Paul, MN
55114. For personal orders, catalogs or other information, write to:
Coffee House Press, 27 North Fourth Street, Suite 400, Minneapolis, MN 55401

Library of Congress CIP Data
Williams, Marie Sheppard, 1931—
      The worldwide church of the handicapped /
      Marie Sheppard Williams.
          p.   cm.
      ISBN 1-56689-047-0 (PBK.)
       1. Williams, Marie Sheppard, 1931- 2. Social work with the handicapped—
Minnesota—Anecdotes. 3. Handicapped—Minnesota—Anecdotes. I. Title.
HV1555.M6W55 1996
362.4'09776—DC20   96-2578
                                                   CIP

10   9   8   7   6   5   4   3   2   1

contents

AUTHOR ACKNOWLEDGEMENTS

Special thanks to Donna and Beverly and Holly for endless patient listening; to Ann Brown for many hours of support; to Cia and Wren and Kristina at Hopscotch House for much constructive criticism and editing; to Lee Ann Engfer, my editor at Coffee House; to Lori Loughney, who took the manuscript to Coffee House Press in the first place, and who gave it its initial edit; to the Wolf Pen Writers Colony; to the Bush Foundation Artist Fellowship; and to Helen Merrill, my agent, who first sent my work to The American Voice and thus started this whole thing.

And finally, thanks to Frederick Smock, who believed in my stories from Day One, and who has been a friend as well as an editor.

DEDICATION

To Fred Gross and Esta Klein Seaton—both of whom saved my life in their different ways; to Dan Ross, my teacher and mentor; to Morgan Blum, in memory; to Megan and Bob Williams, my first and still best critics; and to Myrtle Clara Coplen, who lives in these stories and in the hearts of many, many people whose lives she touched.

THE WORLDWIDE CHURCH OF THE HANDICAPPED

I know two people. Well. Of course I know more than two altogether, but for purposes of this story, I know two.

One of them is a woman. Her name is Evangeline Kuhlman. She is sixty years old, blind, fat, psychic, some kind of alcoholic, I guess; intelligent, kind, and tough; and she has high blood pressure which she attempts to control occasionally with Transcendental Meditation. She says the T.M. really works, but she can't be bothered most of the time.

Do you remember the Little King in the funny papers?—well, she looks something like the Little King: short, bell shaped, larger at the bottom than at the top, feet in flat shoes (high heels trip her) moving along sort of dancingly, seeming just a little independent of her body.

Once I stood at the end of a hallway at the agency with someone else, Barbara, I think it was, a nurse who works with us; she and I caught a brief sight of Vange walking across the other end of the hallway carrying a big bag of groceries, her arms embracing the bag of groceries in front of her, and we both began to laugh together. "What was so funny?" I asked Barbara a minute later. "I don't know," she said. "But something was . . ."

I think it was Vange's feet walking along under her.

Her face is merry; round, soft, blurred, little nose, little mouth, almost always an effect of smiling; if you ask her any time at all how she is, she will say—"Excellent!" You can depend on it. Her speaking voice is a hoarse shout, ruined into this by years and years of talking to blind people who are also hard of hearing. She wears glasses with thick convex lenses through which she can see just a little. A kid said about them once: Lady, how come you wear crystal balls in front of your eyes? Vange was terribly pleased, and told this story all over. Behind the crystal balls her eyes tend to roll around (she has, among other things, an eye condition called nystagmus): the eyes almost never focus entirely, and without much sight they see everything there is to see, or damn near.

She is (she says) crazy. I am pretty crazy too. When we are together we are sometimes marvelously and spectacularly crazy. Technically she is handicapped. Technically I am not.

We work together at a rehabilitation agency for blind people. We are social workers. We work with people who are only blind (very few of those anymore—the whole handicap business has become much more complicated recently as medicine slowly and with incredible selfless dedication learns how to save us all from congenital death and makes senility a state bordering on immortality) and with the deaf-blind, blind diabetics, blind psychotics, blind retarded people, old blind people, blind CPs (cerebral palsy, that is), blind epileptics, blind alcoholics, people blind from M.S. (multiple sclerosis; you probably know this, but I am telling you anyway) and leukemia and Hodgkin's disease and lupus, blind amputees, blind hydrocephalics and microcephalics, blind people with brain tumors and brain cancers, people blind as a result of surgical accidents (and are they ever mad!—but you can hardly blame them, can you?), people blind because of self- and other-inflicted gunshot wounds (these frequently result in full or partial lobotomies—take a tip from a pro, don't ever try to off yourself with a gunshot to the head, it just isn't very satisfactory) and people with every possible combination of the above: blind diabetic kidney transplants with for example amputation and/or neuropathy; once a blind diabetic epileptic with glaucoma; once a fifty-three-year-old black blind diabetic psychotic woman (who had a perfectly encapsulated paranoid system, you don't see that very often, even in psych wards; she came out perfectly normal on the MMPI—Minnesota Multiphasic Personality Inventory—and the psychologist who tested her said he wished he was as sane as she was, which amused us all, since we knew damn well she was nuts, and we were pretty sure the psychologist was too), blind retarded CPs. Once we heard of a blind diabetic transplant with leukemia and a broken leg; this totally cracked us up (you have to be in this business to appreciate the level of the things that keep us going). Well, anyway, are you getting the picture?

II

One night Vange and I sat on the floor surveying the wreckage of a party that we had just held at her house. We were very drunk and very tired. A bad thing had happened at the agency that day, I think it was the time somebody in my department got fired over my head, I believe that was it—so we were also angry and hurt and depressed. And as a consequence of all this, we were hilarious.

Once Greg, who is technically our boss, told us, "You should find your personal friends outside of the field of rehab." "Jesus Christ, Greg," somebody said, "who the hell else could understand us?" That person was right; we are the honorable cadre of folks who look straight at incomprehensible pain five days a week for a living: who the hell else *could* understand us?

"Listen, Vange," I said. "I am absolutely fed up, I absolutely want to get out . . ."

"But where could you go?" Vange said. "Where could you possibly work after this?"

"Nowhere," I said. "This job is the goddamned ultimate satisfaction, which is about to kill me."

"Right," she said.

"Every place else would be boring," I said.

"Anyway, we're too crazy now, no place else would want us," she said, with the cracking laugh that comes from screaming at deaf people for twenty-one years and smoking three or four packs of unfiltered Chesterfield Kings a day. Vange was once on the National Committee for the Deaf-Blind, and everybody hated her for it, as they hate me now for the diabetes program, which has become, if I say so myself, practically world-famous: well, sort of world-famous, we once got a postcard from Russia asking about it.

"Jesus, Vange, we're trapped," I said.

There was silence. Then:

"I could get out," she said.

Me—"How?"

She—"I could have myself diagnosed as an alcoholic or a schizophrenic and collect disability insurance."

We sat there for a stricken and illuminated minute, staring at this new and marvelous possibility.

"Holy shit, Vange," I said. "I could too."

We took off from there. We listed our disabilities, which, when it came down to it, were extensive. Vange said she had a quadruple disability: she was old, blind, alcoholic, and crazy.

"More, Vange," I said. "You have a bad toe."

And me? I am schizophrenic (really, folks, a genuine nut. Visions, voices, the whole swinging bit. You'd be surprised how many of us there are out here and trucking). I am also a woman (a downtrodden minority, even now after years of the women's movement), probably alcoholic, dependent in various ways on various substances, aspirin, meprobamate, antihistamines, B vitamins, strawberry pop . . . I am what we call in the trade an addictive personality, I can get hooked on anything. I cannot yet claim age as a disability, but that too is coming up on me—seven more years of this circus and I can legally claim age as a secondary handicap. And I have a bad back, and the beginnings of arthritis.

"Arthritis, Vange," I said. "You can claim your arthritis too."

"You have brown hair," said Vange.

"Getting gray working here," I said. Giggled.

"And you're short."

"Not *that* short, Vange, I'm five feet four . . ."

"That's short," said Vange.

"You're fat," I said. "Obese."

"Well, you're too thin," said V.

On and on. We reveled in our manifold handicaps. My tendinitis in the right elbow, my upper respiratory infections which I have instead of getting depressed, my depressions which I have when I don't have upper respiratory infections, insomnia (Vange and I are both professional insomniacs), my fear of driving, of getting lost, assorted other phobias, Vange's high blood pressure, my feet, wrecked from pregnancies; I think I am getting hemorrhoids too and the familial goiter. And I am certainly menopausal. And statistically I have a ninety percent chance of being hypoglycemic.

Jesus Christ, when we really looked at it, we were both unbelievably handicapped. We sat on the floor of Vange's living room, amid the party debris, gazing enraptured at the endless possibilities of this new and marvelous vision.

"Think of it this way, though, Vange," I said finally. "Neither one of us is a deaf-blind dwarf."

"A retarded dwarf," she said. "And psychotic."

"With . . ." I choked: "LEPROSY!"

We both cracked up.

"God, Vange," I said, "and can you imagine it? That we are both still working?"

III

There is another thing that happens with us sometimes. We get on the bus outside our agency to go home at 4:30 p.m., when the bus is pretty crowded. Above the long seats in the front there is a sign: PLEASE give up these seats if needed by the elderly or handicapped. And we have our ritual (and to us, very funny; the other bus riders, we suspect, are mainly just shocked) argument over who gets to sit down if there is a seat available.

"I am old, blind and fat," says Vange.

"Well, I'm mentally ill," I say. "And I'm a woman."

"I'm a woman *and* a widow," says Vange.

"I'm divorced, and besides, I worked harder than you did today, and my feet hurt," I say.

"Ok," says Vange. "That last one does it. You are definitely the most handicapped person here." I sit down. I hold Vange's big shopping-bag-purse for her. People look at us, or look away, in disapproval. Not all of them, though. Some of them like us. We do make inroads.

We laugh together; we are entirely enchanted with ourselves.

The situation on the bus gets even more complicated when Peter is with us. Peter is totally blind and carries a white cane. The three of us, having stopped at the O.O. (which is what we call the Orange Onion), are usually a little bit high. Peter (if there are not enough seats for all of us) stands while Vange and I sit. (Why not? He is perfectly all right except for his eyes, he was once a second-string Olympic gymnast on the Lithuanian team, for God's sake.) We laugh and talk together as we always do. People's thought waves, as we get them, are funny: That obviously sighted woman is sitting down while the blind man stands: how terrible!—or, How nice that the poor blind people (PBPs, Vange says; PDSS, Barbara McGuire said once, meaning Poor Dumb Sighted Shit; Barbara—maybe I told you this—was our nurse in the rehab center), anyway, how nice that the Poor Blind People are having such a good time; or—How kind of that sighted woman to be so friendly with those PBPs.

We are all three of us enormously entertained. One night Vange calls Peter a blind drunk, and a woman with a heavy support cane gets very mad at her. "How could you say such a thing to that blind man?" she yells at Vange after Peter gets off the bus and goes trundling down the sidewalk with his white cane tapping. The woman clings to a pole and threatens Vange with her support cane. "That man has class!"

I imagine that we are all three becoming known on the bus as eccentrics. Self-acceptance is I guess hard to take when somebody else is having it; but we keep pushing it anyway, difficult as it is for us, and running as we do the risk of being identified merely as exhibitionists.

IV

A few years ago I took my daughter to an ophthalmologist when she complained of not being able to read signs at a distance. She was fourteen years old. Driving her over, I told her that Dr. Christianson was a good doctor, he was Vange's doctor and Sally Harriman's.

"Vange's and Sally Harriman's!" she yelled at me. "I don't see that *that's* much of a recommendation!" I saw her point: Vange and Sally were both blind.

Dr. Christianson did a refraction, and found a minor degree

of nearsightedness: 20 over 40 in both eyes. He told her that she would have no problem if she wore glasses with a very slight correction. She began to cry, in fact became hysterical. "No! No!" she blubbered; screamed. *"I don't want to be handicapped!"*

Dr. C. was very kind and patient with her, but it was clear that he was absolutely astounded. "You really will be handicapped," he told my sobbing daughter, "if you don't wear glasses, because you won't be able to see as well as you could with glasses."

We got the glasses, but she never wore them, she put them in a drawer, she told no one that she had them.

V

I know someone else. (Remember I told you at the beginning I knew two people? The first was Vange. The second is this man, who also works with us.) This man holds a fairly high position in our agency. His name is Everett. He works as we all do under a lot of stress. He spends a good deal of time lying down in the first-aid room with self-diagnosed sinus headaches. I think they sound more like migraine. He swallows dozens of aspirins and antihistamines. He says he is never sick. What does this mean?

I can tell you one thing it means. It means that he is superior to the rest of us, who go home or stay home frequently with colds, flu, headaches, diarrhea, nausea, generalized funk, and out and out crack-up. I mean, we do a hard job. Why shouldn't we have the small luxury of our illnesses? Everett, I feel, would be much better off if he would come down and join the rest of us in the great army of the justifiably ill.

There is another way in which Everett is superior to all of us. He is a member of the Worldwide Church of Jesus Christ Militant and Triumphant, MaryLou Hoffman's outfit. This church tells him exactly what to believe, so that he doesn't have to stumble blindly through his life like the rest of us, grimly thinking for ourselves.

He tells me he believes that every word written down in the Bible is absolutely literally true. I tell him that I believe this too; and also that every other word ever written down anywhere by any human being at all is true, as is every thought ever thought by anybody; every work of art, every tree, every fucking *rock*—is absolutely literally true. I make no distinctions—James Bond and the Koran—both literally true.

He tells me that white people are superior to blacks because blacks are cursed by God in the Bible; I tell him that it seems to me that we are all cursed by God, or blessed, one way or another, and it amounts to the same thing.

He tells me that men are superior to women because it says so in the Bible; I tell him that I accept this and also that women are superior to men and that they are equal, worse, better, different, the same, everything, all at the same time.

He says that is contradictory and inconsistent. I say, yes, it is, I do see that. And I say that I have no trouble with contradiction and inconsistency, or things that have to fit and don't, I simply believe absolutely everything. I say it is—if nothing else—more fun that way. I say that I have discovered in myself an enormous capacity for belief and I am using it fully; as far as I know this is not yet illegal. *It is so clear to me: if you leave anything out, then nothing belongs.*

VI

One day somebody else came along. I told you I knew two people. Well, as it turns out, I know three. This new guy was a deaf-blind psychotic dwarf with leprosy, and he first showed up in Pittsburgh. He stood on tables in bars (of course he had to stand on tables, he was very short, you could overlook him completely when he was standing on the floor) and he talked to the drunks through an interpreter, a prostitute who had syphilis; since he was not able to speak in intelligible words, as many deaf-blind people are not.

Naturally the message got a little mixed up, but not nearly as bad as another time when he came pretty much as a member of the lower middle class, and a normal—what about those visions, though?—and worked through types who were largely untrained in communication skills.

Well, at first very few people recognized him; I mean who the hell needs a deaf-blind retarded psychotic leprous dwarf?

As it turned out, they all needed him. Gradually, all the handicapped groups fell into line and identified with him. The visible handicaps knelt to him first. Blind, crippled, disfigured—they knew him. He told them to get up on their feet, if they had any, or at any rate to get off their knees.

He spoke in the American Sign Language—ASL; some people still call it Ameslan—which is not the English language at all, which is in fact an entirely different language, and in many ways a much better one. English, while a relatively crude language compared to, say, French, is nevertheless fairly complex and in it you can express quite a few nuances of meaning if you care to try. In this endeavor—trying, that is, to express nuances of meaning—you can get fairly unintelligible.

Ameslan, on the other hand, goes for the gut. It is a feeling language, simple and very beautiful. *I love*—much, plain, or little. *I hate*—the same way. No damn qualifications. Little—if any—metaphor. Straight on. It is common observation that deaf people using this language appear to feel more clearly than hearing people; and do not think as much or as precisely. The language has been described as "freeing." (Well, and consider the freedom of being able to say: I love: without having to go into how or how long or anything else.)

Consider also the difficulties of using a feeling language in a thinking crowd.

So anyway, this deaf-blind guy we're talking about spoke Ameslan through an interpreter. And what the crowd said came back to him in a touch variety of Ameslan for blind people: in other words, the guy had to put his hand on the interpreter's hands while she made the signs. The hazards of misinterpretation were obviously considerable. So you have to take problems of translation into account whenever he speaks here.

He didn't have a halo or anything obvious like that this time around; what he had, actually, was sores, more or less all over his body; they were constantly weeping and bleeding and crusting over into, like crystals. He would stand there on the table, signing to the syphilitic interpreter, and the colored neon lights from the bar—Hamm's, Schlitz, Heineken's, like that—would shine on the scabs all over him and the scabs would catch the lights and would sparkle and glitter, and after a while a poet in the crowd said that this dwarf was covered with jewels.

And suddenly, as soon as the poet saw it, and said it—god!—it was real. Their handicapped hero was flesh and blood covered with real jewels, rubies and diamonds and Tiger-eye whatsits and amethysts and emeralds and glass. Can you imagine it? It went over with the crowd like crazy. Until he took it away.

He wanted to get the message right this time, you see. "No, folks," he signed and the interpreter translated for the crowd, "No, by God, these are real sores. And your eyes are really blind and your ears are really deaf and your backs and arms and legs are really crippled and your faces would stop a bus. *You are what you are.* This is a tough message, and you take it straight or not at all . . . you get it or you don't. . . ."

(Of course, I am translating this into English for your benefit. Before the translation it went something like this: "No, no, no . . . swear me by God. This hurt, hurt real. And your eyes true blind, ears true deaf . . . and your backs and arms and legs true break, not healthy, and your faces much ugly. You real same true you.

Hard news, this. Either accept or reject. Either understand or no. . . ." I could have given you this right off the bat. But I didn't want you to think he was illiterate or something. I give you my word he spoke in a true language: his own.)

Well, eventually they did get his message. They went around looking sort of sparkly, like diamonds, gentle-clear, like glass, and they didn't change at all and they asked for nothing beyond what they were, and they were having a marvelous time accepting themselves and each other.

Then the so-called hidden handicaps came around, when they saw what a good time the deaf and blind and crippled, etc., were having. The diabetics joined, and the crazies, the epileptics and the drunks—they had always thought they were superior because no one could *see* their handicaps, some of the time at least they could fake it as normals, but now they began to understand that it was more fun to be on a level with the others.

Pretty soon lots of people were claiming some sort of handicap: overweight, varicose veins, heart conditions, flat feet. You name it, somebody had it. And practically everybody had *something, some* physical or mental liability, going for them.

Then the character and personality handicaps caved in: the rigid, the cold, the merciless, the shy, the angry, the ones who were afraid, the proud, the loudmouths. After that, the handicaps of circumstance: the rich, the beautiful, the talented, the intelligent, the strong. And all the skin colors, black, white, yellow, red, and all the shadings in between—were declared to be handicaps. And all the sexes and *their* variations—just handicaps.

No formal church was ever founded, because they *were* a church—"The Worldwide Church of Jesus-Christ-All-of-Us-Handicapped." And everybody belonged.

VII

I would like to tell you that it lasted forever, but it didn't last forever of course. In a few years the blind people got the idea that because they were first, they were special. A superiority cult of blind people started up: a sort of subdivision—The International Church of the Blind. The Black Is Beautiful Church came then. And Women's Lib. And Gay Liberation.

What will he come as next time? A woman? Twins? A war? A machine? A concentration camp? A tree?

They remember a prayer he taught them: *jesus-christ-ourselves, save yourselves/itselves/themselves. There is no Other. None will come except it/she/he comes as you.* (The hour was very late in the bar the night he gave them that prayer, it was after closing; and the interpreter was tired and ill; and it may be that the prayer got a little garbled in the translation. It certainly is a very strange prayer. It certainly isn't any Our Father Which Art in Heaven.)

MIRACLE

The subject of this piece of writing is dwarfs. And how I feel about them. I do not feel good about the way I feel about dwarfs; in fact, I feel bad about it. In this particular way, in this small and perhaps irrelevant part of my life, I am unquestionably a terrible person.

(I don't really feel that it is irrelevant, though, you know as a matter of fact, I have begun to believe that it is absolutely central: the heart of it all.)

The way this thing with the dwarfs came about was that I attended the annual United Way picnic last summer when Evangeline Kuhlman from our agency organized the picnic and a record number of people attended. Vange Kuhlman, in addition to being a first-rate organizer, is blind, so I went with her as her driver and sighted guide to the early morning champagne breakfast that started the picnic off. Vange needs a sighted guide like she needs a hole in the head but we thought it was a funny idea and as a consequence I began the day fairly smashed.

Every year the United Way—I suppose you know that the U.W. is a sort of umbrella collection agency that coordinates fund drives for most of the nonprofit charitable agencies in almost every city—anyway, the United Way has a picnic every year in our city. The point of the picnic is that all the agency representatives should get together and get to know each other. People attending are issued color-coded tickets and everyone with one color has to sit at the same table. This is done so that no one will be allowed to give in to any natural instinct to sit with people they already know.

There are also divisions by colors into game teams, softball, races, and what have you, so that you are not only precipitated into enforced conversation—or, at a minimum, sitting mute—with strangers, but you are also obliged to play with them.

This idea in itself has a certain validity, I think, even a sort of charm; but of course it doesn't work very well. For one thing, people can—and do—trade colors, or make deals to get the colors they want. For another thing, I have never yet seen a red—for example—ejected from a blue game and forced to get into a red game. In the clutch, you can always plead stupidity. (Or—this is a joke—*color blindness?*) You can try anything to avoid meeting your mirror image in your fellow man.

None of us are really crazy about the United Way picnic. In fact, few of us are crazy about the United Way—we have to go through such unbelievable hoops to get our yearly pittances—I once said to our executive director: Avery, goddammit, get us out of the United Way and I will personally go out with a can and collect door-to-door for this agency. But we have to go to the picnic anyway. You could look at it this way—it is probably somewhat better than actually working.

Almost all of the agencies that work with the various handicaps and/or disabilities—there are ongoing arguments about those two terms, and I certainly want to touch all bases here, I mean if you are going to insult somebody unwittingly, you might as well make sure that you insult everybody equally—anyway, all the agencies belong to the United Way, so handicapped people were absolutely everywhere at this picnic that I am writing about, which was held at Minnehaha Park. Every kind of handicap you could think of was there: blind people (they came from our agency), deaf people talking in sign language to each other, quadriplegics and paraplegics in wheelchairs or with leg braces and crutches, CPs (CPs are people with cerebral palsy, in case you don't know), both on foot (more or less) and in wheelchairs, retarded people, old people, arthritics, hunchbacks (I don't know what the technical term for this condition is, I guess I should know, this is perhaps another way in which I am less than a good person. Did you know that people who are deaf and who do not speak do not want to be called deaf-mutes? I'll bet you didn't know that, did you? It is very hard to keep up with all the new areas of sensitivity in this field), and probably nuts, drunks, epileptics, and diabetics, although obviously unless you really know the territory you can't spot these last four. Unless they get into their acts, of course.

Every imaginable kind of twisted, tormented, broken, grotesque parody of the idealized human body, and presumably of the human mind, was at that picnic. The cumulative effect was nearly overwhelming—as an AB (Able Bodied) I felt (almost anyone would have felt) surrounded and outnumbered. But I was relatively ok with it.

Until I met the dwarfs. After that, the formulation in my head was: except the dwarfs. The dwarfs, I am very sorry to announce to you, freaked me out. I simply could not relate to the whole concept.

Nobody else affected me this way. Why, I'm even ok with midgets, for Christ's sake, so the thing about the dwarfs made no sense at all. I was looking at all the other people there like they were ordinary people, like me, poor sons-of-bitches just trying to make it through their lives. (I suppose I am in trouble with the women's movement there. It's like there is no way to stay out of trouble these days.)

But the dwarfs I could not deal with. There was something too strange about them. Little people out of fairy tales, magical, fabulous. Terrifying.

I couldn't stand it. The others and me were Us; the dwarfs were Them. No question about it. I am thoroughly ashamed of myself.

They say there was a man once who was afraid of leprosy, in the days when it was not called Hansen's disease. They say God told this man that he would have to kiss a leper if he wanted to stay in the club of the God-Servers. And they say that he did it, that walking along a road one day he met a leper and he embraced the leper's body and his filthy rags and bandages and kissed the leper's disintegrating mouth. And they say further that the leper turned into Christ. I am not aware of anything in the story that says that this man *became* a leper because of that embrace, but I shouldn't think that story would be entirely complete, finished, unless he did.

Do you suppose it could happen that way to me? That God could speak and tell me to embrace and kiss a dwarf? And that I would, for my punishment and privilege—a miracle—*catch dwarfness?*

I am playing softball at the United Way picnic. I am playing first base (in actual fact I wouldn't play softball for any amount of money or persuasion; I was once hit between the eyes with a basketball and had my glasses broken and I haven't played any kind of ball since. No way. But this is a fantasy, anything can happen in it) and a dwarf is up to bat. He gets a line drive toward third and he runs for first. Me. (Oh Jesus no not me don't let this happen . . .) Inside myself I hear a Voice: Kiss That Dwarf. He makes first, he runs right into my arms on his little short legs, his head comes about to my waist, I hug him and pound him on the shoulders and kiss him and say, "Well done, baby!"

No—oh no: you can see that that simply isn't the way it would have to happen: the embrace, the kiss, in that fantasy, are much too hidden and masked, they are part of a game. It is much too easy, there is none of your classical religious torment about it, no Yes Lord—and there is no room in it for me to become a dwarf. Or for him to turn into Christ. (Wouldn't that blow them away at the United Way picnic?)

But some way or other, that way or another, I think it could happen. I think it *should* happen.

A BLIGHT ON SOCIETY

I

Vickie and Grange.

Victorine and Grangeford de los Alamos.

You don't believe those names, right? Already you think I am making this up?

Well, you wouldn't have believed those people either.

Vickie and Grangeford were . . . sweethearts . . .

Yes. That's just what they were.

And listen: don't laugh. If you laugh, I'll—I'll rip your nose off, that's what I'll do.

I'm the only one who gets to laugh.

II

As part of my job at the agency I do intake, among other things. Brenda Pauley, who is a rehab counselor at the state agency—our referring agency—called me one day.

I've got one for you: her sardonic, flat, pained voice came over the telephone. Brenda is probably my favorite counselor over there: she never bullshits me, she shoots absolutely straight, her attitudes are almost a hundred percent negative, I find her very funny.

I've got a woman named Victorine de los Alamos, she said that day. Listen, you'll like her, she said: she's diabetic, she's got some vision left, a lot of other problems, and get this, her husband also became diabetic recently and is starting to lose vision too.

Are they both on Disability? I asked.

The Social Security fund disability section: that's what I was talking about.

Not yet, said Brenda. They will be in a couple of months. Or at least Vickie will. Right now they're on SSI.

SSI is Supplemental Security Income, in case you don't know it. A kind of welfare.

I wouldn't want to shit you, said Brenda: I'm probably the only professional in town who likes them. Vickie's doctor hates them, and their social worker hates them, Legal Aid hates them, Methodist Hospital hates them, listen, their *garbage collector* probably hates them, the *mailman* probably hates them.

I laughed. I know Brenda. I think I do. Why's that, Bren? I said.

Well, you know, she said. They're a multiproblem couple. A blight on society. The sty in the eye of the nation, you should excuse the expression. They've got every agency in town involved in their case. And the thing is, they're not a bit ashamed or depressed or anything. They're making a very good life out of it.

Multiproblem: you have to understand that this was right at the height of the great Multiproblem Discovery. Would you believe it, social workers and such had worked for years with people and until the time of the Great Discovery they had assumed that every one of those people had only one problem each. The notion that some of them had two or more at the same time: say, poverty *and* handicap *and* disease *and* illiteracy: that notion was an absolute mindblower to professionals. And didn't they *love* the multiproblem families at first? Oh, they did, for a while; well, they had a *category* for them, you see. If they put them into the category, they could understand them. This love did not however last: it soon became apparent that even if you knew what to call them, you still couldn't do anything about them. Social workers hate things they can't do anything about.

Well, if you like them, I'll like them, I said to Brenda. Probably. I like them, Brenda says. But you know me, I'm very strange.

Brenda brings them in to talk to me. Vickie—I see on the referral information that B. has handed to me—is fifty-five years old. She is gray haired and quiet. Grange is fifty-four, and awful. (The referral information does not say that, I am just throwing that in for you.) Grange sits hunched forward in one of the chairs in front of my desk: heavyset, florid, mustached, big calculating smile flashing on and off as he psychs me out. Oh, I've seen his kind: I am onto him. He clutches a battered tweed hat in both hands in his lap.

Hello, hello, he says. I'm really glad to meet you. Brenda here, Brenda says you know your onions, and what Brenda says goes a long way with me . . .

Hello, Grange, I say. I'm glad to meet you. And Vickie, how are you?

She's fine today, Grange says. She's really pretty good today. He takes one hand off the tweed hat and reaches for his wife's hand, squeezes it. He turns to her: You're fine, aren't you Vickie? Vickie smiles then; a singularly sweet and piercing smile that reaches out to meet him. I touch Vickie's shoulder: How about if Vickie tells me? I say.

Grange: Oh, Vickie doesn't talk much. She won't tell you how she really is. She'll say she's just fine. I'm the talker here.

Me: Yes, well, I'd really like to get to know Vickie a little. I'd really like to hear it from Vickie.

Grange: Now that makes sense. That makes a lot of sense.

Talk, Vickie.

Oh, Grange is the talker, says Vickie softly. Grange usually talks for me.

Grange gives me his flashing, apologetic, and cringing smile again: that is also merry and impudent. What did I tell you? he says.

I'm kind of shy, murmurs Vickie.

That's all right, Vickie, Grange says. He holds her hand. She smiles at him, that piercing bright smile again: he smiles back at her. We're very devoted to each other, he says. We're very devoted. Two tears squeeze out of his eyes and straggle down the sides of his nose, past his grin.

And now she's blind, he says; and two more tears roll down. God. He looks like a big sincere crocodile. Smiling. Of course I like him, how could I not like him, he is so awful? I look at Brenda as they all get up to go, bundle back into their coats. And Bren looks at me as they leave, her face twisted and sardonic: how about that? the look says. I knew you'd like them. You're as strange as I am. The look says.

I'm going out with Tommy Rizzio these days, Brenda says to me as we walk down the stairs toward the front door of the agency. Had you heard? *Tommy Rizzio!* I say. No. I hadn't heard. Jesus, Brenda, you've got to be kidding, I think to myself. Tommy Rizzio. *Not* a good idea. In my opinion.

III

I saw a lot of Vickie after that, when she came to our agency as a student. At the agency, they teach people how to cope with being blind. I saw her when specific problems came up, or when she just wanted someone to talk to—after a while she did begin to talk— or when I met her by accident in the hallway. She talked about death and Grange. She was afraid to die and she loved Grange.

Afraid To Die I could get my teeth into. Talk to me about it, I told her. Talk to me about death, what does it mean to you to die, Vickie? (What Does That Mean To You—that is a professional phrase, like Mmm-hmm. They teach it to all of us. Actually, I don't mean to make fun of it; it comes in very useful at times; and it reflects a useful idea, that people say things in a way to hide from themselves the real meaning; and that the words lie unless you squeeze the truth out of them.) But Vickie couldn't talk about death. She could only say that she had a great fear, was very afraid. But then she would mention Grange, and the marvelous smile would come, and death would be forgotten for that day.

I was sixteen when I met him, she tells me. He was fifteen. She says that they were married in three months and have been together ever since; she says they have lived in many places, California, Wisconsin, Michigan, trying one venture and another. She says they have never had a real house until now; now they live in a house across the river in St. Paul, and this is wonderful to them.

One day Vickie didn't come to school. I called and talked to Grange and didn't get anything very satisfactory out of him. Victorine's foot was bothering her, he said. And the doctors were really screwing them over, the doctors didn't know what they were doing. He bitched and cried and laughed over the telephone. But he said Vickie would come back to school in a few days.

She didn't come back.

Brenda called me. Look, she said, Grange won't let me talk to Vickie; I'm going out there to find out for myself what's going on.

I asked her if I could go along. Sure, she said. Asking is a necessary formality; the form is that the client always and forever belongs to the referring counselor. Even in Bren's case, I felt that it was as well to stick to the ceremony.

IV

So the next day we drive up to the house in Brenda's car. The house is a neat white rambler affair, with an attached garage. The garage door has an American flag painted on it. Big: it covers the whole door.

Will you look at that, I say to Brenda.

Far out, she says.

Do they rent? I say.

Oh, sure, says Bren.

They never owned anything in their lives, says Bren.

Must be a very tolerant landlord, I say.

We go in. The living room is paneled in mirrored squares that reflect furniture and plants to infinity. Even the ceiling is mirrored. In front of the mirrored fireplace and reflected in it is— Guess. You can't guess? No, not in a million years—a life-size plaster statue of Jesus Christ, painted in bright colors.

My goodness, says Brenda: this is a remarkable room.

Do you like it, says Grange. I did it. I thought of it. I put the mirrors up. I painted the statue.

It's, ah, wonderful, says Brenda. You're very talented, Grange. (That's another thing they teach us in school: Perjury. There's a course in it. I swear to god.)

Oh I love to paint things, Grange says. Of course I bought the statue, but the painting is mine. *Do* you like it?

Oh *yes,* we say. I got an A+ in Perjury. I believe Brenda did too.

Look, I'll show you another one, Grange says. He leads us over to a corner of the mirrored room. On a table is a painted statue about eighteen inches high, this one of two people, a man and a woman, embracing naked, looking into one another's eyes.

It's Adam and Eve, Grange says. His uncertain smile flickers on and off.

Adam and Eve! we exclaim. Goodness.

Grange lowers his voice to a confidential mutter. There's

something special about them, he says. Do you notice anything special about them?

We look. Don't see anything. Grange tips us off: kindly.

Notice Adam's mustache, he says.

Adam has a painted mustache.

Notice Eve's hair.

Eve's hair is painted gray.

Brenda gets it before I do.

It's you and Vickie, isn't it? she says.

Yes it is, Grange says, his hands clasped in front of him, gazing at the statue. It's me and Vickie. I had to have my little secret there didn't I? It just came to me, what I would do . . .

Well—God. What can you say?

I say: It's marvelous, Grange. It's a great idea. It's a wonderful idea. You're a wonderful artist, Grange.

He smiles at me, a big smile full of teeth. Yes I am, he says: pretty good. If I say so myself.

Lord. I am afraid to look at Brenda. I know I'll laugh. I am very touched by the statue but I know I'll laugh anyway. If I look at her. You see, it is in me to laugh at things: life, death, comedy, tragedy, all of it. It is in me to laugh. It is the way I save myself. Do you have a way to save yourself? What is your way? I am really interested in your answer.

V

Grange showed us into the bedroom where Vickie was waiting for us, and then he left us alone with her. Vickie was in bed, lying against heaped-up pillows in a canopy bed. The canopy was made of purple crepe paper: pleated and looped and shirred and scalloped. And set off—*set off?* my god: it needed to be *set off?*—with strips of gold rickrack tacked onto it with goldheaded thumbtacks. The devil of laughter in me began to jump up and down and to choke.

I let Brenda take the lead: What an interesting bed, Vickie, she said.

It's pretty, isn't it, said Vickie. Grange thought of it and I helped him do it. Before, you know.

Before you lost vision, Vickie? said Brenda.

Yes, Vickie said. Before.

What's happening with you now, Vickie, said Brenda.

Oh, it's my foot, said Vickie. My toe.

Well what's wrong with your toe?

Oh, well, it had a blister on it and then it got worse and the doctor said I should keep off of it or it might turn into gangrene and I did keep off it but now it's gangrene anyway I think . . . Vickie began to cry.

Gangrene. I looked at her, lying on the heaped pillows in the purple crepe-paper bed, a gray-haired, faded, strong-looking middle-aged woman. Who had gangrene. Who lived in a house of mirrors, whose husband painted her as Eve on a plaster statue.

Oh, you know, the laughing devil in me loved it, the devil went mad. Purple crepe-paper bed canopy, he pointed out, and gangrene! Too much. Too much.

This was the point at which I could have hoped that Brenda would take over—after all, Vickie was her client. But Brenda dropped out on me. She sat in a bentwood rocker by the window and the sun streamed in past white starched ruffled cotton curtains and lighted her: a smart and attractive woman, thirty or so, blonde short hair exquisitely cut, beautiful restrained figure in tasteful clothes, and unwilling apparently to say the next thing.

(I will never have Brenda's style. I *try;* god knows I do try; but I always end up looking like a refugee from a garage sale. "Funky," people say. They also say—the nicest ones, the ones who actually like me, and not everybody does—the ones who like me say that I have my own style. I take some consolation from this idea.)

So it was up to me. God—was this fair? I was the one who saw everything so goddamn funny: what could I say?

Oh, well, I did know what I had to say. It did come to me: things do. In the clutch, things do come. That's where the training figures in.

Is it death, Vickie, I asked. Is it that you think you will die of this?

She nodded a little and the tears came faster and became shaking sobs.

I sat down next to her on the bed, I took her in my arms and held her and smoothed her gray hair.

Cry, Vickie, I said. It won't be all right, this is not going to be all right, I won't tell you that, but you can cry anyway, and maybe that will help some . . .

I looked over at Brenda, who was still sitting in the bentwood rocker. I motioned to her. She got up and came to the other side of the bed and sat on it and held Vickie from that side. So there we were, two fortunate cynical women, holding a sobbing Vickie with her gangrenous toe under the purple crepe-paper canopy.

VI

Brenda and I are both divorced. It is a bond between us: one of many. We both married the kind of man that fortunate cynical intelligent women often do seem to marry in this society nowadays. They even write books about us: *Smart Women, Foolish Choices*. Titles like that. Each of us has a daughter, Brenda and me, I mean. Brenda's daughter is eight years old. My daughter was eight when the divorce occurred.

Why, Mama, my daughter pleaded on the day of the divorce. Why did you do it?

We don't love each other anymore, Margaret, I said. I don't love your Daddy any more. He doesn't love me. We just can't live together. . . .

It's not true! she said. It's not true.

It is true, Margaret, I said.

But the thing is, if I couldn't live with Bud, who the hell could I live with? Nobody? Maybe nobody. Maybe I just don't have it in me.

Margaret plotted for years to get me and Bud back together. Her plots were sinister and extraordinary. I watched her with amazement: that she was capable of such calculation, manipulation.

She also plotted and planned to keep other men out of my life. In this plotting she was more successful.

One night at two a.m. I was in a clinch in the living room with a guy named Jason O'Fallon. I don't suppose I loved him, but I did like him, in a way: he amused me: and he touched me: he was so sad and crazy. Margaret came down the stairs in her new Christmas robe and snapped on the overhead light. O'Fallon and I jerked out of our embrace and stared at her: she was beautiful, thirteen years old, standing on the stairs. She accused us with enormous brown eyes: *What exactly,* she said, staring over me at O'Fallon, *are your intentions toward my mother?*

I couldn't help it, I laughed. And I gave her an answer. Margaret, I said, O'Fallon wants to screw me and I want to save O'Fallon's soul.

Well, O'Fallon was horrified: my god, he said. Good Christ. And that was pretty much the end of that romance. There was an occasional phone call or drop-in visit after that; but basically it was finished. Well, you see, she made me see him funny.

When she graduated from high school—she was living with her father in Santa Monica at the time—I went out there for the ceremony. As the three of us walked on the Santa Monica pier after the graduation, Margaret came between Bud and me and put an arm around each of us.

She sighed—*ahhh-h-h-h:* and I knew something awful was

coming. The white carnation that the headmaster had given her as he sent her forth into the world dangled delicate from the fingers of the hand that she rested on my waist. This, she said, smiled, sighed on the warm summer night air: *this is the realization of a brokenhearted eight-year-old's dream . . .*

Yes, honest to god, she really said that.

Oh, Margaret, for god's sake, I said.

No, it really is, she said. You believe it, don't you Daddy?

Bud smiled at her in hopeless infatuation. My beautiful, beautiful daughter: he said.

See, the thing is, I did him some harm too, in my quest for, what do they call it, Self. Maybe we could have worked it out. I wonder if we could have worked it out.

No. Never. That was not an answer. What is an answer? I don't know. There are questions that have no answers. Maybe this is a question with no answer.

VII

As I hold Vickie, sobbing, in my arms, I am thinking of: Bud, Margaret, the mirrors, the Jesus statue, O'Fallon, Brenda's ex-husband whom I never knew. He was a bastard: that was all she ever told me about him. I don't know, Brenda was probably not all that easy either. None of us are, these days. You know *us:* the cynical strong intelligent talented women, fighting tooth and fucking nail for our rights.

I held Vickie and rocked her and murmured words to her, and Brenda held her and was silent. After a while:

Talk to us about it, Vickie, I said.

It's, it's, they might have to cut my toe off, she said, snuffling.

You've been so brave about it all up to now, Vickie, I said. Why now? This?

This is the way it starts, she said. With one toe. Then they cut off your foot.

That might happen, yes, I said.

You die then, said Vickie. They cut off more and more, and pretty soon there's no more to cut off, and then you die . . .

Is it pain that you're afraid of, Vickie? I said.

No, said Vickie. Not pain.

Is it what happens to you after you die that scares you so, Vickie?

No, no, that's all right, God takes me home, I'm not afraid of that . . . She trembled and sobbed in my arms.

What then, Vickie?

Oh, she said, oh, it's that I have to go alone. It's that Grange can't come with me . . . I have to leave Grange alone . . .

So that's it. So that's it. Something so far outside of my understanding that I feel my mind stretching into a whole new shape to get it in: the sentimental idea of love. The real for Christ's sake thing. Love. In a middle-aged gray-haired woman with a gangrenous toe under a purple crepe-paper canopy made for her by a fat and tasteless grinning oaf. On Welfare.

Oh, my devil who saves me is laughing to split his sides: can you hear him? Surely his laughter is so loud that you can hear it.

(Saves me?)

VIII

Grange walked us out to Brenda's car. The red-white-blue garage door dazzled in the sun.

Thank you for coming, he said. It means a lot to Vickie that you came.

Thanks for letting us come, said Brenda.

Think nothing of it, he said.

Your garage door is spectacular, Grange, I said. Did you paint it?

Oh! Yes! he said. I change it for every holiday, he said.

Every holiday? I said.

Every single one, he said. And sometimes I put in one for a holiday no one would ordinarily think of, the summer solstice for example. If I happen to want to. Vickie's birthday.

It's a marvelous idea, I said.

Yes, isn't it? he said. Isn't it marvelous? Isn't it just marvelous?

IX

So we drove home, Brenda and I. We were quiet for a while. She drove along the freeway back toward the agency. The traffic got heavier.

Then: Christmas, I said. A big red Santa. *Plus* a nativity scene.

And listen, Halloween. A big orange pumpkin.

Ghosts! Skeletons!

We started to laugh. Washington's birthday! Cascades of laughter. Thanksgiving! A Thanksgiving turkey! Arbor Day! Trees! On the, on the *garage!* And listen, gallons and gallons of *paint!* The taxpayers are buying *gallons of paint* for this project! Oh if they only knew, god if they only knew . . . listen, Valentine's Day . . .

God. It's a wonder we didn't hit another car. Out there on the freeway.

It's a wonder we didn't get killed.

Valentine's Day.

X

We don't talk about it very often, Brenda and I. Once in a while. But it is there connecting us: we have an important connecting memory.

Brenda brings me news of them sometimes.

Grange and Vickie have moved to Wisconsin, she says. Vickie is going to a rehab center there. The state counselor called me to ask for our records . . .

One day: Vickie's had her foot amputated.

And another day: Vickie died, Brenda says. Grange called me.
How did he sound? I say.
Like always, she says. Full of, you know, *life* . . . I mean, *sad,*
but kind of energetic . . .
I wonder what will become of him, I say.
I wonder, she says.
Last week, I met Brenda for lunch. She is in the process of
getting her second divorce: from Tommy Rizzio, who turned
out to be a bastard too.
I told her that I was going to write a story about Vickie and
Grange.
Will you let me read it? she said.
Yes, I'll let you read it, I said. Sure.
Maybe I will. Maybe I won't.

I don't know, I am a taxpayer too, and I feel that my money was
well spent in that case. And, thinking about it, suddenly I see
myself rushing forward to embrace my death, my only lover: my
promised end, my goal, surcease. Lord, sometimes I feel like a
member of the poor: I feel like I need to be on some special
kind of Welfare.

SEQUEL: THE DWARF COLLECTOR

I wrote a very short story recently, a sketch really, about the dwarfs at the United Way picnic.

I showed it to a few people: Sarah, who is a social worker like me; Vange, who works with me; my shrink (I shouldn't call him that, I do it only to be obnoxious and hip, actually he is a very nice man named Fred—well, you knew that somebody pretty good was holding me together, right?); my good friend Maeve; Annette at the agency; and some people in Atlanta. And me, of course.

I include myself in the list because I write all my stories more or less in a state of trance, never knowing what is going to come out, and I feel that I come to the stories when they are finished almost as a new reader: I personally liked the dwarf story, but my critical judgment said it was a total loss from a literary standpoint.

All the other readers had their separate responses to my story; and the thing that interested me most was that they all thought it was about something different—I mean, it was like none of them read the same story. And the responses, some of them anyway, were quite violent. I was fascinated by this phenomenon: I must have done something more here that I don't know about, I thought, to provoke such a diversity of interpretations and such strong opinions. I mean, they could have just said: I don't like it;

or I don't understand it: couldn't they? But they *did* understand; but they all understood something different.

Vange said it was a serious and beautiful story, a sort of parable. Sarah shouted with laughter all the way through, and said it was a hilarious "in" story, a social work story, about how all social workers have *some* weakness, *some* category of people with whom they do not work successfully—maybe fat people, maybe alcoholics, maybe drug addicts—and how they all feel great guilt over this, and harbor a sneaking suspicion and fear that they will "catch" whatever it is in others that they reject the most.

Maeve (whose son-in-law is handicapped—a paraplegic—and who knows a particular dwarf as a person) read it without cracking a smile, in fact she began to look more and more like she was swallowing lemon juice. I had told her about Vange and Sarah's reactions: I waited for her pronouncement: Maeve is very important to me. She said, in a tight little voice like a scourge, "Well . . . I think Sarah was right to laugh . . ." She hates it: I thought. But she never said so; she never said anything beyond that one sentence.

But just last week I told her I was going to write a sequel to the dwarf story that I knew she had disliked, I was going to do so because so many odd things were happening as an aftermath of that story—and you know, she denied, not that she had disliked it, *but that she had ever read it.* Now, Maeve is my friend who remembers everything, this was very odd.

"Do you want to read it now?" I asked. "I happen to have it with me."

It seemed to me that there was fear on her face, in her voice: "No," she said. "Oh, no. What if I still didn't remember it? Or didn't remember it again? Oh, no." The story stayed in my purse.

I took the story to Fred, the shrink; I told him about the other reactions. He read it without any comment or smile and handed it back to me: "I think Vange is right that the story is a serious attempt," he said. "But it certainly is *not* funny. It doesn't come off at *all* as a funny story."

(That was the day we were talking about God and messages, and like that; poor old Fred tries to hang in with me, he tries hard in spite of all difficulties; and I had left my cigarettes in my coat in the outer waiting room and went to get them while he read the story. His receptionist was just telling someone that Fred was "in session," but when she saw me come out she put the call through.

When I went back into the office—I didn't find my cigarettes, they were in my purse all the time and I didn't see them—Fred was just hanging up the phone. "Well," he said, with the rather guarded smile that I hope he doesn't reserve just for me, "things like that make me suspect the existence of a divine providence after all."

"I keep telling you," I said.

When I showed the story to Annette, who is one of the secretaries at the agency, she laughed until she cried and had to grab some tissue off my desk and mop at her eyes and blow her nose. "It's marvelous!" she said. "It's absolutely marvelous . . . you attack *everything,* it is an attack on *everything,* women's lib, the Catholic church, the handicap racket, the United Way—god, *everything,* I *love* it!"

The people in Atlanta (Elinor, who used to be my freshman English teacher in college and still harbors hopes that I will pull away from this bizarre deviation into Social Work, pull up my socks and become a writer—her writer, obviously—and her husband Anthony and their friend Justine who is also a teacher of writing) came to the story as to a foreign land: the land of rehabilitation, the land of The Handicapped, about which they knew nothing.

They all loved it, but their appreciation was literary. This astonished me, because as a writer I felt that if the story failed more miserably on one front than on another, that front was the literary aspect. In fact, I felt it was close to anti-literature.

My friends wanted more about the United Way picnic, though. They wanted me to tell them more about the strange new country they had never heard of before, the strange country of rehabilitation. (I am reminded now that before I went to work for an agency for blind people, I had never known a blind person, I had no idea that the woods were simply full of them; now I can't walk on the street or take a bus ride without seeing several people who are blind. We edit out, I suppose. A crazy person sees whatever is there and adds to it, perhaps, and a sane person erases from what is there whatever he or she chooses not to see?)

I said to Elinor (I knew the answer before I asked), "You don't like the mystical dimension of the story, do you?"

Elinor had a funny look, a funny smile, for a second, like a child caught at something forbidden. Slowly, painfully, like the tin man in the Wizard of Oz needing an oilcan, she shook her head. No. Said no word.

"*I* do," said Justine. "I think that aspect *makes* it." I liked Justine, I thought she was a great critic, extremely intelligent and astute.

II

Something has happened that is strange: since writing that story, I have somehow become a collector of dwarfs. All the people who have read the story, that is, have begun to see me as a dwarf collector, and they keep phoning me or coming into my office to tell me about a new kind of dwarf they have seen. And most of them insist that they have never seen a dwarf before. I myself never saw a dwarf before the United Way picnic. Now, because of that story—what else can it be?—a small segment of the American population is suddenly seeing dwarfs all over the place.

I cannot have increased the number of dwarfs in the world. But can it be that I have inadvertently raised people's dwarf consciousness? So that they can now see the dwarfs that they looked at and erased before?

I know that I did not choose to become a collector of dwarfs; and I am somewhat uncomfortable with the position.

I complained about it to Vange one day. "It does seem a little morbid," she said. But she laughed; in some sense at least she clearly thought that it was a very funny thing to have happened to me. Vange laughs at almost everything. But she does not laugh at pain. So I deduce from this that what I have done (accomplished? created? The field is so new, I hardly know what words to put to it) in the area of dwarf awareness is not wicked or cruel. But what then is it? What have I done?

The way it happened was this: the same day I wrote the story and read it to Vange, I went downtown with her to buy a wedding present. For Annette, as a matter of fact. Walking down an aisle in Dayton's, we saw a dwarf. The dwarf was walking along like anybody else, with a full-size adult person. I think the dwarf was male—but what I *saw* was just dwarf. I poked Vange. "Look," I said. "My god. A dwarf."

Half an hour later we were walking along Seventh Street and the same dwarf appeared. I grabbed Vange's arm. "Vange!" I whispered. "There's that dwarf again!" I was beginning to feel really strange about it, like God was materializing a dwarf to follow me or something.

"It's a different dwarf," said Vange.

"No, I'm sure it's the same one," I said.

"I think it's a different dwarf," said Vange. "But it does seem odd, doesn't it? We never saw a dwarf together before . . ."

"I have never seen a black dwarf," I said—to somebody. "I wonder if there are any." Three days later I saw a black dwarf. In the bus depot.

Then the landslide began. I walked into the paperback book exchange. The first book I picked up was a book titled *The Dwarf.* It was by Pär Lagerkvist, who had won the Nobel Prize with this book in 1951. I bought it. What else could I do? I read it. It was a very strange book.

Sarah called and told me that she had seen a retarded dwarf. Annette came into my office, all excited about her marvelous trophy, and said, "Joan! I have a dwarf for you! I saw a dwarf selling used cars on television! Honest to God I did!"

"Oh my God," I said. "That's wonderful, that tops them all . . ." I was simply stunned. What was the message that I was not getting? I felt like a cat owner who has just been presented with a dead mouse. But you have to admit that there is something intrinsically arresting about the idea of a dwarf selling used cars on TV. What next? Sleeping Beauty in a coma in Hennepin County Medical Center being kept alive by life-support systems? Cinderella as a janitor in the agency? I tell you, dwarfs belong in fairy tales; for all of me, they should have stayed there. I am getting more and more freaked out about this.

The only person so far who hasn't come up with a dwarf is Fred. The *shrink?* Think about it.

Even Maeve became part of the thing at last. She and I were sitting last week on a stone bench in the Radisson Arcade downtown, and what should walk past us but the smallest dwarf imaginable. A dwarf woman—I am getting better at this, you see, I also saw a woman—certainly no more than three feet tall, probably smaller than that, with tiny metal braces on her tiny crippled legs, and walking along very deftly on the littlest pair of crutches I have ever seen. She was with a normal-size woman, who towered over her, and they were chattering away, just like anybody.

Well. I did stare after them when they had passed. But Maeve was the one who had the big reaction. She said softly, with tears in her voice—who was she apologizing to?—"I'm sorry. Oh, I'm so sorry. I know I'm staring . . ." That was the point at which I told her I was going to write a sequel to the dwarf story she had disliked so much. And when she denied having read it, and became frightened at the idea of reading it then and there.

But Maeve did say, later: "I couldn't tell what age she was, could you?" Age! I had just gotten to sex. Maeve is way ahead of me. Maeve sees more. She always has.

Elinor called from Atlanta yesterday. She reported that she had gone to an all-night pharmacy, the only one that was open, in a very bad section of Atlanta; and had seen a female dwarf prostitute. "She wasn't really very short, though," Ellie said, sounding apologetic. "Maybe about four feet." Well, I am getting resigned to all this. "It's all right," I said. "Four feet is acceptable. And prostitute is really terrific . . ."

Can you see the implications of all this? *Dwarfs are real.* And if the world is full of dwarfs and I never saw them before, and now I can see them and so can a lot of other people, what *else* is out there that I do not see?

Where is this going? I wonder if anyone ever went over the edge on dwarfs? And if *I* should go over the edge on dwarfs, what would be on the other side of the edge?

I mean, freaking out on God or LSD is one thing, but freaking out on *dwarfs?*

There I would be, the only full-size person among hundreds of millions of dwarfs. Would they see me? They might not see me.

POOR RAYMOND

One of my former clients is named Raymond. About once a month—which shows admirable restraint in the circumstances, I think—he phones me or Barbara at the agency and asks us to kill him. For a long time now, I have made a joke out of it (Raymond can take this, he understands me, I understand him, we are both very tough people, there is some love between us). I tell him that I can't kill him, that the United Way (which helps to fund our agency) simply wouldn't approve of this kind of service.

Raymond means it. I know he means it. Barbara knows he means it. I don't know what she tells him when she takes the calls. I imagine she handles his request very much as I do; she and I worked together so well for so long that we almost became the same person.

We did intake together; intake in our agency is a very fancy operation indeed because our clients have so many complex medical problems. I bailed out of that job three months ago; I am still at the agency, but I do a different job now. One way of looking at this is that I abandoned Barbara. Another way of looking at it is that I saved myself. However you look at it, there are tag ends left over from the old relationship. Raymond is one of these tag ends.

We report Raymond's calls to each other, or leave notes about them in one another's mail slots, since we no longer share the same office. Barb: Raymond called. Joan: Raymond says if you have the time will you call him. Barb: Raymond in U. Hospital, says will you please call?

Sometimes we call back and sometimes we don't. I mean, we do get irritated with Raymond. This has been going on for so long. Everybody is so tired of Raymond's suffering.

Barbara and I discuss it. We laugh. Understand terrifying pity in one another. Poor old Raymond, we say. He'll never die. He will, though, of course. Eventually.

Raymond is blind. He has diabetes, has had a kidney transplant (his brother Leo donated the kidney that keeps Raymond alive; Leo now feels great regret and guilt about this, but how could he know what would come of it?), had first one foot amputated just above the ankle, then the other, then the first leg amputated above the knee. The last time we saw him, he was in a wheelchair, and was pushing the chair around with the one hand he has the use of now, and the stump of the longest leg. One of his elbows has an ulcer that breaks open and drains more or less constantly. He has a terrible temper, and is extremely demanding (a pre-trauma character trait, I am told.) He was an Army officer in World War II. Knowing Raymond, I imagine he thoroughly enjoyed the war.

He was hospitalized with something like pneumonia recently. (Which was just awful. He called to tell me he was in the hospital. His voice was very faint. He said something like: *Glug, glug, glug.* I was in a hurry, I was impatient, I said, Speak up, Raymond, I can't hear you. He whispered, or gargled, sort of, I can't speak up, that is why I am here, I have fluid in my lungs, I can't talk through it very well. Oh Christ Raymond, I said, *I'm sorry. . . .*) Just now he has had a stroke, which has left one side of his body paralyzed and has impaired his speech. For seven years this has been going on—ever since the kidney transplant. If he had not had the kidney transplant he would have died seven years ago. But of course seven years ago he did not want to die. So he had the kidney transplant.

Last week he called me, and I had dammit had enough. He said, laughing as always (there is nothing maudlin about Raymond, he is in many ways obnoxious as hell, but he is not maudlin), *I still want you girls to choke me you know. (Girls*— Raymond is, among his other unlovable attributes, a dedicated chauvinist. God. He sounds awful, doesn't he? Well, he is awful, but there is something about him . . . something . . . that makes him, not likeable, god knows, but admirable. Even lovable. I guess we love him, Barbara and I.)

I threw in the towel. I said: Raymond, I hear you. I hear that you want me to kill you. But I can't. *I just can't do it, Raymond.* In the first place, something in my conscience that I don't understand won't permit me to do it. And in the second place I am chicken. But I want you to know this: If I could do that for you, I would.

Well, he was very pleased. He said: you mean that, that if you could do it, you would?

Yes I would Raymond, I said.

That means a lot to me, he said, to know that you care enough about me to do that for me if you could.

I described this conversation to Barbara. She listened to the whole word-for-word report: *He said, I said, then he said . . .*

Then: It's the thought that counts, she said.

Well, we absolutely cracked up. I guess we laughed for ten minutes straight. Until we cried. Oh ho ho, it's, ho ho, the THOUGHT, hoo woo, gasp, choke, giggle, that COUNTS! Screaming: IT'S—oh god—THE THOUGHT—doubling up; people think we have a wonderful time in social service— THAT COUNTS—Christ Jesus, how is this bearable? I wonder if anybody laughed like this at the original crucifixion? Probably not. I mean, that event probably didn't take long enough for laughter to become inevitable, necessary, appropriate. Three hours is nothing much; human beings can watch agony for three hours without cracking up. Tears maybe; grief; pity; shock; anger; prayer; indifference; embarrassment; indignation; but not the deepest feeling, not the last terrible understanding, the final freeing laughter, the final sanity.

But there were certainly some openings for humor in the original production—I mean, take for example *Father forgive them for they know not what they do;* surely that is a funny line? Surely that line has some potential to crack somebody up sooner or later?

You want to be a social worker, a therapist, serve mankind and rake in the chips? Be a fat cat? You can be my goddamn guest.

II

When I was about sixteen, my parents bought a little dog for my brother Arden's eleventh birthday. We named the dog Skippy, but we called her Guppo.

She was a very loving, very faithful little creature. Sometimes our father, who had a violent temper, treated her badly—but she loved him anyway. She loved all of us.

She barked hysterically and fiercely at all friends. Once when a burglar broke into the house at night, she didn't make a sound. Somehow we liked her for this bad judgment—it made her seem more like one of us, our family, as screwy as the rest of us. We all make rather remarkable mistakes too, and are dear to one another because of the mistakes.

Guppo got old, and we all (the children) grew up and got married and moved out of the house. One day I came home and my father was holding Guppo and Guppo was huffing and puffing away and rolling her eyes. I never saw my father cry for any of us, but he was crying for Guppo.

Joan, Guppo is sick, he blubbered. Guppo can't breathe.

Now, I am the only member of my family with any common sense at all. (Some people who know me might find this an extraordinary statement, but they don't know the rest of the family.) I said: That dog has got to go to the vet.

I can't take him, my father sobbed. (We get confused about the sex of our animals, and about many other things.) I'm afraid the vet will put her to sleep, he said.

I'll take him, I said. I said: It has to be done; you can surely see that it has to be done.

So my father drove the car and I held poor miserable drooling Guppo in my arms and carried her in when we got to the vet's.

How old is she, the vet wanted to know (no fool, that vet—he knew she was a female and stuck with it) after examining her very quickly and gently. How old. I figured it out. I am also the only one in the family who can think in the clutch. Well, I figured, Arden was eleven when we got her, so I was sixteen, and now I am 32, so she must be sixteen years old.

The veterinarian was very nice, a very gentle and kind young man. He explained to us that in dogs' years Guppo was extremely old. He said she was having a massive coronary attack. He said he could probably bring her out of it this time, but that she would never have a very good dog's life again. He also told us that she had cataracts on both eyes and was probably nearly blind.

He was so gentle, that vet. And so concerned—for us and for the dog. He made it easy for us. He helped us to understand that the choice was ours; he helped us to understand that if we loved her we would let her die, be free.

So we did decide that she should die. And it was an easy choice; what kind of monster would choose suffering for a loved animal? I held her in my arms while the vet prepared a lethal syringe, injected it. I don't know what I expected, but certainly I did not expect what happened. In the space of half a breath, in the blink of an eye, life was gone from that suffering little body. I held in my arms a warm, limp remnant; the life was released and gone.

There was something absolutely ok about it. There was something really nice about it.

My father and I did not talk as we drove home. I was sad, but very peaceful, having done what I felt was certainly right. As we drove up to the garage, my father said—god, he sounded so touched, and so impressed—he said: And they do for an animal what they won't do for a human being . . .

He never got over it, he talked about it for years, in a gentle, awed, wondering tone of voice.

III

A lot of people blame the doctors for the weird thing that has happened in this culture; they say the doctors force people to stay alive past the point at which nature and God intended them to die. But it is not entirely the doctors' fault, you know. It is also partly your fault; you and the doctors are in collaboration. In the days of your youth and health you have told the doctors that you want to live forever, you pay them to study more and more so that you can live for one more day, one more year, at any price, at any cost, with any pain; you do not of course know what the pain will be. You keep contributing to medical research. You keep paying taxes for it. You are crazy; and they (the doctors) are, I think, the helpless, caught creations of your terrible insanity. Of course, as members of humankind, the doctors are also insane; I said it was a collaboration.

Why do you want to live forever? For heaven's sake, call up your doctor on the phone and say that you have made a mistake, you have changed your mind, you don't want immortality on this earth after all.

Or I suppose you could learn to laugh; maybe if you can laugh you can stand immortality; to want to be immortal on this earth surely is a funny and laughable longing? Surely it is a very comical idea?

IV

My cat got leukemia last winter. The vet called me at the agency when he had the diagnosis and told me the score, said it could be treated, said remission was possible, blah, blah, blah. But he also said the cat was depressed and in pain. He told me to take a few days to think over what I would do; he knew that I loved that cat; why, I had seen that cat through at least eleven lives, I had more medical bills invested in that cat than I have in my daughter.

It took me not a few days but just an hour to decide. It nearly killed me to do it, but I called the vet back and asked him to give my cat death that night. The vet stayed after his regular hours to do it.

Sometimes I wish I could kill Raymond. Sometimes I understand why he can't choose to kill himself—he is afraid he will go to hell, Christ, can you top that one?

Sometimes I understand and sometimes I don't. I guess I am something like you—I am afraid to call the doctor. But I did call the vet. Maybe I can work up to it yet.

Maybe someday I can say (and put my money where my mouth is): *Stop this.*

EMONT STERNICK SAYS HELLO ──────

Well. So. Emont Sternick. Yes.

An unbelievable fellow: *what he did* . . .

I'll tell you: maybe you won't believe it, but I'll tell you anyway. What else is a storyteller for? A storyteller tells stories, and
is not believed. Oh, well, for a little while maybe: in what they
call—you know about this—a suspension of disbelief. A suspension of disbelief, I think, is a momentary flash of light: rejected
afterwards.

Suspension of disbelief is not belief. But I'll tell you anyway.

I was walking down the hall by the cafeteria at work one day
and Jeannette from the sewing department stopped me.

Tell Vange Emont Sternick says hello: she said.

What? I said.

She said it again: Emont Sternick says hello. Tell Vange.

Tell Vange I can get, I said. And *says hello.* But what is that
other part?

Emont Sternick, said Jeannette. He used to work here.

A person: I said. I asked Jeannette to wait while I wrote the
message down on a piece of paper; you have to understand that
I am one of those people who forget everything; I learned early

that I have to write things down if I am not going to forget them. Emont Sternick says hello, I wrote on the piece of paper. And: *Tell Vange.*

But Vange wasn't at work that day, so I couldn't tell her right away and get rid of the message. The message stayed in my jacket pocket. It kept bubbling up from there into my mind. Emont—Sternick—says—hello: Emontsternicksezello. It became a hum in my mind, a mantra.

Emont Sternick Sezello. Suddenly it became conscious and clear and I stopped what I was doing (fortunately I was only sitting at my desk in my office with the door closed shuffling papers, a very important activity these days) and laughed. A regular attack, I had: Emont—haha—Sternick—hoho—says, says—choke, cough, shout, giggle, wipe eyes—HELLO!

It was wonderful. It was a terrific high. Why, I couldn't keep it to myself. I got our tutor, Patsy Aaron, on the phone and asked her to come into my office. Immediately Patsy, I said: I have something wonderful for you.

Patsy is very good about my urgent summonses; she came in right away.

Listen, I said: Patsy, listen, I was walking down the hall by the cafeteria . . .

You're kidding, Patsy said. You mean there's an actual human being with that name?

Patsy is entirely reliable in this way, I can depend on her always.

Yes, I said: I mean no, I'm not kidding. And listen, Patsy, listen, he, he, SAYS HELLO!

I choked on that, I could hardly get it out.

God, what a message, she said. What a name. I don't believe it.

I showed her the piece of paper from my pocket. You have to believe it, I said: it's written down.

Oh, it's true then, she said. And laughed and laughed.

Absolutely came apart; and I came apart with her. Sitting in my office, she and I went to pieces over this message written down from Emont Sternick.

When we pulled ourselves together we got down to the real business of it.

That name, said Patsy, has possibilities.

Me: Oh, right. That name has, well, actually—um—greatness. Wouldn't you say?

She: Sex appeal?

Me: Oh definitely sex appeal.

She: Can you see it in lights?—"Starring Emont Sternick?"

Me: Star of stage screen and RADIO!

Listen, said Patsy, what about this: *The Emont Sternick Peace Prize!*

Oh, *right!* I shouted. And listen: The Emont Sternick Foundation!

Emont Sternick slept here, she giggled.

Mein Kampf, by Emont Sternick, I said.

Oh, wow. We cracked up.

Emont Sternick rides again! she said. Who Was That Masked Man, I said, and we went off.

Oh, we had a simply marvelous time. Joy sparkled on the ceiling of my grubby office.

We kept it up all day. I would stick my head in the door of Patsy's office: The Emont Sternick Award, I whispered.

She poked a note under my door: *Was E. S. a Fraud? asks National Enquirer.*

All day long, meeting in the halls: Hi, Joan, Emont Sternick says hello.

Emont Sternick Says Hello. Just try it. Doesn't it make you feel warm all over? Loved? Finally recognized? I mean, say it a few times. Get into it. Can it hurt you?

When Vange came back to work I gave her the message: Vange, Jeannette said I should tell you that Emont Sternick says hello, I said.

Oh, said Vange, pleased: Was he here?

Well, I don't know that he was *here,* I said. But Jeannette must have seen him somewhere, and he said hello to you.

Well, isn't that nice, said Vange. Dear Emont. Only she didn't say Emont, she said something more like Amen.

Amen? I said. I thought it was Emont.

Well, whatever, said Vange. It's a Lithuanian name. Amen is Lithuanian. He came over from Europe about the same time as Peter did. Peter is blind; I think maybe I told you that before.

So was Emont blind? I said.

Oh, no, said Vange. Amen can see.

Well, who was he, I said. I mean, what kind of person was he?

Is he, Vange corrected me. If he left a message, I assume Amen is still with us. Somewhere. I'll have to ask Jeannette.

Ok, *is* he, I said. What kind of person *is* he?

Well. I guess I don't know any more, said Vange. It's been so long ago . . .

Oh, Vange, I said: for heaven's sake. What kind of person was he *then?*

Why do you want to know? said Vange. I mean, you sound *so interested.*

Well, I *am* interested, I said. I get off on his name.

Well. He was. He was just an ordinary person, I guess, she said. Who worked here.

Oh, honestly, I said: You know what I mean.

He worked in the old sewing department, Vange said. He was a foreman eventually. I thought he was quite attractive. He had a beard. Everybody said he was having an affair with Audrey Billings.

Audrey Billings? An affair with Audrey Billings? A dumb name like that? God. I was furious.

Who the hell is Audrey Billings? I said.

Someone else who worked here, said Vange. How nice that Amen said hello.

I found the real Emont Sternick completely unsatisfactory.

I pursued the definition of Emont Sternick with Peter. Peter, what was Emont Sternick like? I asked him.

Immons was a real character, said Peter.

Immons? I said: I thought it was Emont?

I expect you are not giving it the real Lithuanian pronunciation, said Peter, in his own accent: *High eggs baked Q R nod . . .*

How do you spell it? I said.

Oh, it is impossible to spell in English, said Peter. Em-paw-zee-bool.

Audrey Billings called him Nick, said Peter. She couldn't pronounce his name either.

Audrey Billings! I said. *Nick!* I said. *Either!* I said. *Either!*

I was really annoyed. Peter laughed at me.

Have you got a fixation on Immons? he said. *(Hev Q godday feex . . .)* Immons would be pleased. Immons was quite a ladies' man.

Oh, Emont: I am losing you.

Reality testing is a downer.

Listen:

Emont Sternick Avenue.

Sternick's Third Law.

The Sternick Principle. The Sternick Theory. The Categorical Imperative of Emont Sternick.

Almond Sternick stew.

Illman Starnick.

Allman left to your partner . . .

Oh, this could take you anywhere. Over the Edge with Emont Sternick: Emont, wait, don't go, I am coming with you! You and me, Emont; just the two of us . . .

Patsy too? Oh, all right, Patsy too. Not Peter. Not Vange.

Father, Son, and Emont Sternick.

There was an item in the local paper one day: the Barnesville Star. This is what the item said: *A man identified as Emont Sternick was found dead this morning of unknown causes in a furnished room at 1936 26th Avenue South in our fair city. The room had been rented three weeks ago under the name of Wallace O'Leary.*

I didn't know him, said the caretaker of the building, Ms. Emma Stolz: he came late at night, I was nearly asleep, I never really saw his face.

A bankbook in the dead man's pocket revealed a deposit of nearly a quarter of a million dollars. Heirs are being sought.

Gee, I wouldn't have known it, said Ms. Stolz. He seemed like such an ordinary person.

What would she know? What would the *Star* know, that lying rag?

Emont Sternick, as I know from secret messages found in corked bottles floating in perilous seas, is alive and well and sitting on a park bench in Sternick's Corner in Portland, Maine. Also, he phones me from time to time, Emont does.

Audrey Billings, my foot. She was never anything to Emont.

I will have to be careful, however, about Patsy. Emont Sternick has a wandering eye for younger women.

Actually, in many ways a monster, Nick. But a marvelous lover. Sex appeal—oh, yes. Definitely.

RAYMOND AND THE RIP-OFF: OR, WHY I WRITE STORIES

I told you something before about Raymond, how he calls the agency and asks me and Barbara to kill him, do you remember? Well, this is a different story about Raymond, this is the one I intended to write in the first place, but that other story happened, and had to be written first. It is like the stories own me, they push me around, it is almost like I have nothing to do with it.

This is the way it works: stories happen to me. Once I got into this storytelling, I began to notice that stories were happening. And when a story happens, I have to drop whatever else I was doing and write it down. Sometimes the story that interrupts turns out to be a good story and sometimes it doesn't. This does not matter at all. What matters is that it gets written.

I think stories happen to everybody. I wonder what becomes of people when they don't write the stories down, or tell them, or pay *some* sort of attention to them. Perhaps the stories stay somewhere in their eyes, the eyes that saw the stories in the first place. Maybe after a while they have so many stories in their eyes that it is like having cataracts and the people begin to see things strangely through all the mixed-up stories, one story laid upon another, each story changing the one under it, and on and on. Maybe the people are in a way crazy then.

It seems to me that if I write the stories down as they happen and as they want to be written, I will not have to see as strangely as I think I would if I didn't write them. I don't know if I will ever catch up, though; there are so many stories left in my eyes from my whole life that I would I think have to receive a special dispensation to stop living for a while and just write down the stories.

Because as long as I keep living, stories will keep happening. So you see I can never catch up. But maybe I can stay even with it; not keep any *more* stories in my eyes, not see any *more* strangely.

Writing a story as it happens, seen through the prism of strangeness that is already there, is like having a film removed from my eyes. Afterwards, it seems to me I can see more clearly for a little while.

II

I took a few days off from work last March to visit my friends Elinor and Anthony in Atlanta. But the day before I left, Barbara and I decided to go out and see Raymond. Barbara is a nurse, as I may have told you before, who worked with me until recently in the program for blind diabetics at our agency. She and I set up the program together, and it was a very good program, largely because when we started we were too ignorant to know how we should have done it. It is still a good program, but now Barbara is doing it with someone else. She is also doing intake with someone else; I kept the administrative end of the job, the supervision, the community ed., the I and R—Information and Referral—for example. I am now called the manager of CRS—Community Rehabilitation Services.

Barbara is very torn. The diabetes program is absolutely involving, consumes anyone who works in it. But Barb has also got a husband and a house, two dogs and a couple of teenagers; between these two poles, the diabetes program and her life, she is daily stretched.

From the outside, it looks very uncomfortable. Barbara's voice has an edge in it these days; she is a fine and capable nurse, but the endless strain is beginning to tell. I can remember how it was when we ran the program together; it was terrible but it was also wonderful—we saw ourselves as the Mutt and Jeff of Rehab, two do-or-die comrades on some incredible front line, making a little island of light, holding back the terrible darkness of human agony just a little, just a little longer. No kidding, it really felt like that—it is a wonderful thing to be able to remember. It is also wonderful to be out of it.

Raymond is a leftover diabetic double amputee kidney transplant from the old times.

III

When you do special things for people, those people I think tend to grow on you and become more important to you than they would otherwise be. In fact, I think that is the way one kind of love happens. The special thing Barbara and I did for Raymond was that each of us met him at the door when it was our day to work (we job-shared at that time), and we met him together on our overlapping Wednesday. We held his wheelchair while he transferred out of a taxicab and then we wheeled him into the building, got him on the elevator and upstairs, and then he was on his own.

That was absolutely all we did for Raymond; but somehow that was enough. The thing is, he couldn't have come into our program without this small service. And no one else wanted to do it—nobody felt that it came within their job description. We never worried about job descriptions, Barb and me; we just did whatever needed to be done, wacky as it may have been. So we wheeled Raymond in and up every day, and we got to know him very well in those few minutes a day. We knew his courage and his obnoxiousness, and his (rare) moments of letdown, weakness. We really liked Raymond. No one else did. He was so goddamn much trouble.

When he got out of the hospital after his last siege—a stroke—his wife called and asked us to come out. So we took a couple of hours the morning before I left for Atlanta, and we drove out to see them.

IV

We expected things to be bad, and they certainly were. Raymond was up out of bed for our visit, and in his wheelchair. Since we had last seen him, he had had one leg amputated higher up than before, just below the knee, and the docs had finally given up on prosthetic feet and legs—Raymond just doesn't heal anymore—so he was pushing the wheelchair around by poking at the floor with the bandaged stump of his longest leg. The stroke had affected his left side, his arm on that side was nearly useless, hanging over the armrest of the chair; he could use only his right arm to help propel the chair. The upshot of this one-sided, two-pointed approach to wheelchair travel was that he could mainly just go in circles.

He was frantic with rage. Raymond was a crazily independent sort of person so his helplessness made him almost insane. But he was still in there trying, going in circles. And he was yelling at his wife to help him. Furious also because his speech was slurred (the stroke) and even his yelling wasn't particularly effective. His wife, Belle, whom we had never met before, looked to be right at the edge of a breakdown. Quite a nice house, typical suburban.

A teenage son was vaguely around. At one point he stuck his

head in through a door and said hello, and grinned. His grin was Raymond's. It touched me right at my center, somehow, that grin.

Well. We waded in and took over, the nurse and the social worker. First we talked with both of them together, Raymond and Belle—that turned out to be plain useless. They were both so angry and so focused on their separate anger that they talked over each other—she shrilled and he shouted complaints, each about the other. A hysterical, hopeless bickering.

—He doesn't sleep all night, he keeps me up all night.

—That's a lie, she's lying!

—(To us) I am not lying, he never sleeps . . .

—I do sleep, I do. She's lying!

Well, you can see how far this was getting us. So finally Barbara stayed with Raymond and I took Belle into the bedroom and talked to her. It poured out, all the anger, all the grief and resentment, how tired she was, how much she wanted out, how the priest said she had to take Raymond home from the hospital AMA(Against Medical Advice) because Raymond wanted to quote die at home unquote. (God, how I hated that priest. And the worst part of it was, he left town before I got a chance to rip his ears off his head. I wish some of these humanitarians had to take care of the results of their decrees, their legislation.) She talked about how difficult, how impossible Raymond was now, what a wonderful man he had been, how they had loved each other, how it was all gone now and she wanted, only wanted, Raymond to die, Raymond to be away from her, from them.

It's just terrible for our son, she said. The other day, Raymond was yelling at us and Randy said, if you don't stop yelling I'll lock you in your bedroom.

Good for Randy, I said.

But that's terrible for a son to have to say that to his father, she said. That's terrible.

Yes, that is terrible. What could I do? I gave her a back rub, made her stop talking, made her rest for a few minutes. I think it helped a little. I think human touch helps, even when it is a stranger's paid touch.

I could go on and on about this, but what's the point? I mean, you've got it, haven't you? The only thing we could do was talk Raymond into letting a night nurse come in so Belle could sleep. Forget about nursing homes, forget about hospitals, and forget about Raymond dying—if you are thinking that these solutions are possible, that I am making a big thing out of a simple matter just to write a story, the only thing you are revealing is your naïveté. The system in this country doesn't work like that. In fact, the system doesn't work worth a damn. The suburbs are full of Raymonds.

V

We were so depressed, Barb and I. We took a long lunch hour at the CC Tap after that visit, and we each fed our depression a couple of vodka martinis. Then we went back to work to finish out the day.

I told you I was going to Atlanta the next day? I had taken a hundred dollars out of the bank for spending money, and that night I discovered that the money was gone. Ripped off or lost, I suppose.

Now, under normal circumstances, an occurrence like this would have sent me into a total decline. I am perhaps the cheapest person alive, or certainly a leading contender, anyone who knows me will tell you that. And I have a really terrible hang-up about money—I keep telling you that I'm crazy, but the truth is, crazy is ok, it's neurotic that's difficult—anyway, if I haven't got enough money, I don't feel safe. And I never have enough, there *isn't* enough anywhere, so of course I never feel safe. Losing *a hundred dollars* would normally be like getting hit on the head with a two-by-four. I mean, I would normally be really upset.

But that morning with Raymond had done something weird to me. It was like something had broken loose in my head, snapped forever. It was like nothing, *nothing,* mattered, could ever matter again, compared to what was happening in that house. I just didn't give a damn about the money, in fact I felt really cheerful about it, freed. I went to the bank again the next morning, on my way to the airport, and I took some more money out of savings, and that was all there was to it. It didn't bother me at all, I could care less, if I had no money at all that wouldn't bother me either. I felt euphoric, light as air, like a big piece of excess baggage had been thrown out of my head, like I could float, or fly.

I was all full of it when I got to Atlanta. I couldn't stop talking about Raymond and the theft of the money and how ok it was that the money had been stolen because it didn't matter compared to Raymond.

You'd think I would have bored them to bits in Atlanta, right? But as it happened, it fit right into something that was going on there. Anthony (Elinor's husband) has an inoperable heart condition, and in effect has been told that he is dying, has not got very long to live—like maybe next week. That also did not matter to me—compared to Raymond.

Elinor and I had been planning to go to Greece together the following June; she told me that this was of course off now because Anthony might have a heart attack. Maybe San Francisco in December for a couple of weeks would be possible. She said. Maybe Anthony could hack that.

I might be dead in December, said Anthony.

Right, I said: Then we'll go without you. Ok? Cheery as hell, I was. Well, think about it, what were my choices? To mope with him? And it just didn't matter to me, you see. Compared to Raymond's being alive, Anthony's dying was a perfectly ordinary and acceptable event.

Well, they kind of caught it from me eventually, Elinor and Anthony. In a funny sort of a way, I really think it was very good for them—that someone thought it was just ok for Anthony to die, no big deal. He really came out of his depression, started talking about the things he wanted to do before he died. I don't suppose it lasted, things like that rarely do, but temporarily I think it gave them a lift, me being so offhand about Anthony's dying.

I really did feel that way too; no fake about it. And they believed it because of the money. I mean, if *I* didn't care about getting ripped off for a hundred dollars, they really believed that the thing that made me not care was important. We were all very happy together, we were high for five days, it was a wonderful time.

I didn't care about losing the money, I didn't care that Anthony was dying, I didn't care that I would die. I was free. I think I must have been crazy, a little.

But not neurotic.

VI

The last day of my visit, Elinor and I went to the supermarket. I picked out a few things and stood in line at the checkout. Ahead of me was a well-dressed, obviously prosperous man. I figured that five dollars would about cover my purchases, so I got a five-dollar bill out of my purse, to be ready for the cashier.

The man ahead of me picked up his sack of groceries and left. Suddenly the cashier saw something on the counter in front of her.

Is that yours? she asked me.

I looked where she was looking. There was a crisp new five-dollar bill lying there. It couldn't be mine, I told her. I knew this because I was sure that I had only one five, and that was the one in my hand.

She picked up the five-dollar bill from the counter and ran after the man who had been ahead of me. She caught up with him just as he was putting his groceries into his car, which looked very new and expensive. She spoke to him, he checked his billfold, and she handed him the five.

She came back. She said: You were right, he said it was his.

Then she rang up my items. Three-sixty-five, she said. I began to hand her my five-dollar bill and at that second I noticed that what I held in my hand was only a one-dollar bill. I opened my purse to get out my five and—of course, you know this, don't you?—there was no five there.

It was my five-dollar bill that the man got.

A woman behind me in line chose that moment to say, in that great Atlanta accent, just as the truth was dawning on me: Well, this has made my day: to run into an honest person!

What could I say?—Madame, your day has been made by running into a damn fool?

I choked, said: Oh, I think there must be a lot of honest people left in the world. And kicked myself mentally. And fished out a ten from my purse and gave it to the cashier, who made change and handed it to me.

I put the change into my purse. Picked up my bag of groceries. Walked out to Elinor's car, she coming along just behind me.

Well, I mean, I was pissed. I was absolutely in a state of absolute shock. I sat for about two minutes in silence while Elinor drove out of the parking lot, started home.

Then I took a deep breath: Ellie, I said, you are not going to believe what just happened to me. And told her the sorry tale.

Well, of course she laughed, she thought it was completely hilarious. And (she said) you mean that just as you realized what had happened, the woman really said that, about being an honest person? That really happened?

Yes, I said, it was just like that.

God, she said, that is the funniest thing I've ever heard: you are the only person I know that things like that ever happen to, that must be why you are a writer, because things like that happen to you.

Oh, is that what the problem is, I thought to myself.

But you can see what the *present* problem was: I couldn't even discuss how utterly pissed and upset I was, because I had sold her so totally on the idea that nothing mattered, especially not money, because of Raymond.

But I *was* upset. I think I was beginning even then to get back to normal. Now I have been home and back on the job for a couple of months, and I am completely myself again: I worry about money, I don't feel safe at all anymore, I am sorry that Anthony is dying, it seems important to me. And deep down, I am probably as afraid of my own dying as the next person.

But maybe tomorrow another story will happen, and I will have to stop everything and write it down, and then maybe I will not be afraid any more, for that little while.

THE PRETTIEST GIRL IN EAU CLAIRE

Melanie Wright came back to us again a few weeks ago. Sometimes they come back. We tell them all that they can come back if they need us: if for example they lose more sight; or if they forget what we taught them and need a review, a brushup; or if they change their jobs or whatever and need another skill, or more of something—more braille, more abacus, Nemeth Code, whatever. But out of the hundreds, really very few ever come back.

"We" are the people who work at an agency for the blind. "They" are the people who are or become blind. Obviously we exist because of them—live off of them, if you care to look at it that way. Sometimes we do look at it that way, when we are being particularly honest, or bitter, or even just smart-ass. ("Live off of"?—there are days when I think that if this is living, you can—uh—have it.)

What I remember best about the first time Melanie came is something that was said by John Ellison, who had lived in her hometown, which was Eau Claire, Wisconsin. John was also a client of ours at that time: a diabetic, and blind because of the diabetes.

John said: "I remember Melanie. She was the prettiest girl in

Eau Claire. She could have had anything."

John ought to have known; he was a mailman and he saw a
lot of people. Also, if he was then what he is now, he had a good
eye for a pretty woman.

A good eye? A blind man? Well, what else can you say: I mean,
be reasonable. Why, John has even been known to flirt with me.
And I am forty-eight years old to his thirty or so. Meeting me in
the hall at the agency, he will say sometimes, "Hello, Beautiful,"
or "You look wonderful today, Joan."

How would a blind man know? Why, what difference does
that make? I am flattered anyway. And believe—a little. Enough
to make a bright spot in a dull day sometimes.

When Melanie came to us the first time, maybe seven years ago,
she was sixteen years old, and just recovering from surgery for a
brain tumor. Her blonde hair had been shaved off for the
surgery and was beginning to grow back in wispy tufts. She
wore a kerchief to cover it. The brain tumor and the surgery had
left her partially blind and brain-damaged.

Her parents came up from Eau Claire with her. They were
ordinary people, confused by what had happened to them. It is
tawdry I guess these days to say "heartbroken"; but this is a
tawdry sort of story coming up—at least I think it will be like
that. So I shall say that the mother and father were heartbroken.
We convinced them to trust us—what else could they do? Take
her home, hide her?—she had to learn some way to live.

The mother and father both cried when they left her with us.
She did not cry, though. The prettiest girl in Eau Claire?—the
looks were gone: there were instead the great scar, the tufts of
hair, the round, china-blue eyes (who knew what they could see?
no ophthalmologist was sure; these brain cases are almost always
impossible to really get hold of) staring in shocked bewilder-
ment, the slack face, mouth half-open, speech impaired—halting,

words turned around, slow, groping. But the manner of a pretty girl remained; she was imperious, like a little queen. Demanding, my god; it was as though she simply did not grasp yet what had happened to her. And remained absolutely convinced that she deserved something quite special that could not be defined.

We did the best we could for her, but it wasn't really very much. We couldn't do much. Sometimes we can't do much. And to tell the truth, we weren't that crazy about Melanie. We tried hard for her because we are, in our own field, the best in the business. But there was something about her you couldn't quite like; another social worker, Vange Kuhlman, said it—that Melanie was unformed, unfilled; she was like a glass bottle, clear, delicate, stuck at sixteen, empty—no mood of hers in the shifting maze of sixteen-year-old moods was really her; Melanie was no one. But all the shimmering, changing charm was still there, the sixteen-year-old promise that would have become— what? who could tell? who could possibly tell?

"The prettiest girl in Eau Claire"—the phrase stayed with me for seven years. Came back to me at odd times, sometimes for no reason at all, sometimes when I saw John Ellison, who stayed on with us as a teaching aide.

Sometimes word would filter back to us: Melanie Wright, remember her? she is living at—wherever; Melanie Wright is working as a physical therapy assistant, she's doing pretty well. It always felt unfinished.

Melanie must be about twenty-three now.

She called again a couple of months ago. Asked for me. "I—I— w-want—to come back—Mrs.—Shep-Shepherd—" the soft, thin, charming voice came over the wire, clear as glass, broken.

"I'll see what I can do, Melanie," I said. "Why do you want to come back?"

"I—have—"—long pauses all the way through—"lost—more—vision—M-Mrs. Shepherd."

"I'm sorry, Melanie," I said. What else can you say? There is never anything even remotely adequate.

"Thank you, Mrs. Shepherd," Melanie said politely. That was a characteristic thing about her. She was always extraordinarily polite and formal. And very, very neat and clean. Meticulous, even: as befits the prettiest girl.

"What are you doing now, Melanie?" I asked. Just prolonging the conversation, just not liking to quit with the feeling that I was talking to no one.

"I am," she said in that high flute voice, "witnessing for the Lord, Mrs. Shepherd."

Witnessing for the Lord. Ok. "That sounds good, Melanie," I said. For inadequate, you just can't beat me some days.

Pause. I could feel the broken synapses trying to come together. Then—"It—*IS*—good—Mrs. Shepherd," she said firmly.

Christ. Christ Jesus. Witnessing for You, is she? And what do *You* look like? What fumbling, stumbling words do You speak to us in? I get mad; god I get mad sometimes.

When she came in again as a student, to study the compensatory skills all over again (braille, abacus, typing, Techniques of Daily Living, leisure time activities, and Orientation and Mobility—did you know that there is a master's degree given at six universities in the United States in Orientation and Mobility?) it didn't take long for the teachers to decide: Melanie is worse, they said, she is— that awful medical word—decompensating.

I don't know, I thought she was about the same—perhaps it was simply that in seven years of living, you expect some change, some growth, and there was none. She was still hollow, like an empty bottle, which, struck, may give off a lovely clear tone, but which beyond that presents little that holds the interest. There just wasn't much in there that you could call—a personality.

I'll tell you something else—my style of thought is humor, and there just isn't anything about Melanie that is funny—I can't hit my own style with Melanie, I can't find a way to tell you about her, she is absolutely elusive, I can only ramble on, hoping to get to something to explain why she haunted me, to justify my feeling that there is somehow a story here and not just a title.

One afternoon at four-thirty I would have been leaving for home, except that I had promised Vange Kuhlman that I would see to it that her client, Rose, got to the bus depot by six o'clock. Rose was waiting by the employees' exit of our building, inside the door, with her suitcase.

"Hi, Rose," I said. "Vange sent me to make sure you got off all right."

"Mrs. Kuhlman not going to stay with me?" said Rose in her soft Southern voice, disappointed.

"Mrs. Kuhlman is on vacation today, Rose," I said. "You remember, she told you that."

"I sure don't remember that," said Rose. We don't ever know for sure what goes on in Rose's head: retardation, craziness, or straight guile. We like her anyway, there is something appealing about Rose, everyone falls for it.

"I'm sorry, Rose," I said. "You'll have to make do with me."

Rose brightened. "Well, that's all right then," she said. "I like you too. I like you as much as I like Mrs. Kuhlman."

I laughed. "You don't have to go overboard, Rose," I said. "There's no reason you should like me. You don't really know me."

"I do like you," she said earnestly, simple duplicity in every intonation, "I like you as much as I like Mrs. Kuhlman."

"Ok, Rose," I said.

Melanie was down there that day too, also waiting for a cab. And Emily Barron, and Jim Wilde. At four-thirty the cabs were already half an hour late; they were ordered every day for four o'clock.

I think you have to know something here about what a trial the cabs are to us: sometimes they are early, sometimes they are late, sometimes they are on time; but often when they *are* on time, the drivers don't know which client they have come for, and just take whoever happens to be there. And then, ten minutes later, another driver comes for the person who is gone already, and that driver is angry about losing a fare. Or something else goes wrong. And someone has to sort out whose fault it is— because if it is *our* fault, if someone forgot to phone and cancel a cab or something, the driver can claim a fare and charge for it even if he drives no one. We have to beg, cajole, plead, conciliate the cab drivers and the cab company—because we are absolutely dependent on them to take our clients home. We can't afford to let them get mad at us, because then they might not come at all. It is a peculiar and abject position to be in.

Why don't we get a van and drive them home ourselves, you want to know? That's a very reasonable question. Listen, *don't* ask reasonable questions, you are just going to confuse the whole issue. Take it from me, try to believe me if you can, we can't drive them home ourselves because we can't, that's all. The laws governing rehabilitation in this country are so incredibly complicated that it's almost impossible to do anything at all while you are trying to observe the laws: the state can pay for cabs, that is within the law. But it won't pay us the equivalent of cab fare. Just don't ask questions.

Now I want to get back to the day I waited for the cab on account of Rose. At four-thirty it is time to begin to call the cab companies. Until four-thirty we can hope that the clients will begin to call the cab companies themselves, after all our major function is supposed to be to make blind people as independent as possible; but at four-thirty the building officially closes. Anything can go wrong at that point; and whatever staff member happens to be there last must resign himself or herself to staying there with the clients until the cabs come.

That day it was me—normally this would not any more be my job at all, because I no longer work in the rehabilitation center, I work out in the community—but Vange has one last client in the rehab center before I pull her out completely for community work, and I went down because her Rose was there waiting for a cab.

"Ok, gang," I said. "Who takes what cab?" It turned out that Jim took Village Cab, which is a suburban outfit, and the other three were waiting for Checker Taxi Service.

"Who knows Checker's number?" I said. Melanie supplied it. I dialed. Got the recording that said all the lines were busy. Waited. Finally got a real person.

"Thank you for calling Checker Taxi," said a surly, harassed female voice.

"Hello," I said. "This is Joan Shepherd. I am a social worker at the Center for the Blind. Three of our clients are waiting here for cabs that were ordered at four o'clock. Can you find out what's going on? The cabs are for Rose Fleming, Melanie Wright, and Emily Barron—B-A-R-R-O-N."

"Just a minute," said the voice. "I'll look it up." I waited.

Then—"Are you at 26th and 38th South?"

"Yes," I said. Jesus Christ, where the hell else would I be? There is only one Center for the Blind in this town. They damn well know where we are. The thing is, they hate us. Or maybe, like everyone else, they are afraid of us, afraid of blindness, blind people, they would rather not drive our clients.

"Just a minute."

Then—"We have all those orders. We're running a little behind today. They should be there in about ten minutes. There's one on the way now . . ."

"Please do your best," I said. (I am always pretty polite on the first call.) "The building is closing now, and one of these people has to catch a bus out of town."

Then we waited some more. Staff members came along, stopped to chat for a minute. Left us. Emily's advisor came and went. I felt a little pissed: you should have stayed, was the thought in my mind. Emily is so fragile, you can't expect her to handle this by herself. Now I'll have to get Rose off and wait with Emily.

Fifteen minutes. Emily begins to cry softly. I go over to her, I put my arms around her. "Come on, Emily," I say. "This is nothing. This is just the way it is." She smiled through tears. She said, "I know, I don't know why I am crying, it's silly."

Emily is about forty years old, she has spent most of her life taking care of her father, who according to reports around town was a rather extraordinary man. He died at the age of eighty about a year ago. Now, when Emily is at last free, she has become blind as a result of her diabetes. The diabetes is very volatile. Silly to cry? Not so, Emily. Cry all night, make rivers with your tears—I have to make a point with you, though, it will not help, tears are not silly, they are just useless after a while. And people do not like you when you cry all the time.

No goddamn cabs.

I called again. A plea this time. Listen, *please,* it's way after hours here, two of these people are severe diabetics who need to eat on schedule and one is meeting a bus. *Please.* (Up against an adversary like the cab company, you throw in everything you've got.)

Five minutes. There will be a cab in five minutes. Then others will come. Really. Honest.

Oh sure. I believe you.

Jim calls Village. Late—they are running late.

Why? It isn't raining, for god's sake. It isn't snowing. I can understand late when it's raining or snowing. But today? With the summer sun shining? Another thing is, another reason the cab drivers don't like us, is that we don't tip, the state (which pays for the cabs) cannot find a way to authorize tips.

I look at Jim. He looks funny to me. I have eight years of experience in the diabetes program behind my eyes. "Are you ok, Jim?" I ask.

"Could you—um—possibly get me a Coke?" he says. Right.

"Sure," I say. I marshal my troops. "Rose, you stand by the door. Emily, don't get shook, I'll be back. Melanie, if somebody's taxi comes, make the driver wait." I run upstairs. The machine is out of Coke. I get a can of Orange Crush. Anything with sugar in it.

I come back. Give Jim the pop. Open it for him. See that he's drinking it. Jim is lucky, he has a lot of warning before his reactions. Some of our clients go into insulin reactions without a second's notice, that is when you have to take over the thinking for them, force the sugar in.

(He's *lucky*? Jesus, I mean you won't believe this, but I just heard what I said—wrote—I mean I just really *heard* it, and I am cracking up right here at the typewriter; I certainly wouldn't dare to cry, my god I might never stop, so obviously I will have to laugh instead. We laugh a lot on our jobs at the Center. *Lucky:* twenty years old, married, infant daughter, mother and father hysterical with grief and guilt, family relationships in tatters, brittle diabetic, retinopathy, kidney involvement, glaucoma, God knows what's ahead—he's *lucky*? All things are relative, I guess. We begin to think in very peculiar terms after we've been here a while.)

I sat on the stairs with Melanie. Late-leavers walked around us. If the person coming down the stairs was blind, we shifted out of the way.

Melanie began what we call a "searching" movement with her head. *Searching:* the head bobs up and down, moves from side to side, twists at odd angles; searching looks very odd, almost spastic, but the explanation for it is very simple: in some conditions of vision loss, the field of vision is fragmented, or cracked, or spotted: the head moves and the eyes remain stationary in an attempt to find and focus upon some object that they want to see.

What is she looking for? I thought.

She found it; she reached out and put her hand over mine.

"It's—kind—kind of—*fun,* isn't it, M-Mrs. Shepherd?" she said.

Fun. "Well, I don't know about *fun,*" I said. "It's ok, I guess. We're all in it together . . ." Apparently that was good enough, because she turned her luminous, vacant smile onto me.

I watched Emily. She was going to start crying again, as sure as god made apples. I was tired. I got up, went over to her, said, "What's happening, Emily?" Slow tears started down her cheeks.

"I'm glad my father is dead," she said. "He thought the world was a gracious place. I'm glad he didn't see this. I'm glad he didn't see a world where cab drivers won't pick up blind people . . ."

So they didn't fool you, Emily, with their talk about *late.* "Listen, Em," I said firmly. "I agree with you. The world is going to hell in a basket. But that's the way it is. We all have to live with it the way it is . . ." My god, I thought, if that's true I'll kill myself.

But this was the way we had all agreed to treat Emily: tough. In some cases it's the only way. We all agreed.

But I have a funny kind of mind; I was suddenly thinking— what if nobody tried to do anything about "the way it is?" What if everybody, always, had "just lived with it"?

I chickened. I put my arms around her. "Emily, I had a father too. I am also glad that my father is dead . . ."

Jim's cab came first. "Hooray!" he shouted. "Hallelujah!" sang Rose. "Thank God," I said: "one down and three to go."

"Whoop—whoop—ie," said Melanie carefully.

I asked Jim if the Orange Crush had been enough, if he would be all right. "I'll be all right," he said. The driver came in to get Jim while Melanie held the door; obviously this guy had driven blind people before, he knew the sighted-guide technique; he led Jim, he did not grab him and push him. In this business one thanks God for small favors. We watched Jim get into the cab; we watched the cab drive off.

Now it was only Checker Taxi that we were waiting for. It was five-fifteen. I decided to get a little tough with the cab company; I called again and mentioned that I might be calling Mr. Willman in the business office in the morning. "A cab is coming *right now,*" a voice (male this time) said. "It should be there *right now.*" Sure enough, a Checker Cab pulled up.

I said to Emily, "Emily, can you hold out a little longer?" Ordinarily I would have put her in the first cab, but Rose was going to miss her six o'clock bus if she didn't leave soon. I explained this to Emily.

"Of course, Joan," said Emily. Appealed to on someone else's behalf, Emily is usually all right. So Rose got the cab. I whispered last-minute messages to Rose (whispering in a hopeless effort to "Observe Confidentiality," for god's sake): "Now, Rose, Vange *expects you to be back on Monday for sure. She says you promised and she believes your promise.*"

Dumb Vange. "I be back," Rose vows. "I promise Mrs. Kuhlman, I be back Monday for sure. I just go see my little Annie."

She may be back and she may not; Rose is from no place in particular, from many places in the South, Mississippi, Alabama, we don't know where else; she is one of a migrant family; lying (or making up fairy tales) is a way of survival for Rose. I hugged her. "Have a good time, Rose," I said. Then she was gone.

The Wisconsin county where Rose lives now is going to take "Little Annie" away from her. As the county should. Rose's sister was murdered recently. Rose's brother slashed his arms with a razor blade from shoulder to wrist in some sort of celebration of this event. Little Annie—who may be anybody's child—four years old, saw this, saw the blood, ran into the street screaming, screams now in her dreams, apart from that does not speak at all. Of course the county should take her away. But Rose is ours, we love her, it is hard for us to know that sometime soon we will have to say: we cannot recommend . . .

The fans that pull in outside air were turned off by now. The air inside was getting hot and stuffy. Melanie wanted to go outside and wait. Emily did not want to budge from the wall she leaned on ("Listen, Em, sit down on the bench"—"No, no, the cab will come soon, I want to be ready . . ."). I had no real choice; I had to stay inside with Emily: the phone was inside and I might need it again, and Emily was too weak to open the door for me if it should happen to lock, which it would if I were accidentally to let it close all the way. And Emily would sure as hell panic if she was left in there alone.

The waiting went on.

Finally at five-thirty another cab arrived. I went outside, held the door open a crack, asked the driver who he was for: Melanie, he said. I wedged my purse in the door to keep it open, what a great idea why didn't I think of it before—yelled at Emily that I wasn't leaving her, and then whispered to Melanie around the edge of the building—"Melanie, I know this isn't fair, because this cab is really for you, but will you please let Emily have it?"

"Cer—certainly, Mrs.—Shepherd," Melanie said. I touched her shoulder, shook it a little. "Thanks, Melanie," I said. I went inside. The driver came in with me. "Emily, your cab is here," I said. Emily burst into tears and laughed at the same time.

"Come on, Emily, sweetheart," the cab driver shouted. He took her hand and placed it above his elbow; my god, he even knew sighted guide! I blessed his name, whatever it was. "Come on now," he said. "None of that. We're going to have a lovely ride!"

Emily laughs; you can hear the young girl in her laughter. "Oh you!" she says. Then they are gone, Melanie and I are alone.

"Melanie," I say, "I want you to know that I think you are a nice person."

"Why—is that—Mrs.—Sh-Shepherd?" she says.

"Because you let Emily have your cab."

"I—I—was *glad* to do it, M-Mrs. Shepherd. I felt—*kind*."

I keep my purse wedged in the door. I mean, you never can tell, we might need another call to the cab company.

We are so tired. We are so bored. We decide to sit down on the cement walk outside the building, side by side, leaning up against the building. Suddenly Melanie says, "If you weren't— here—I'd be—alone . . ."

"Don't worry, Melanie," I say. "I'll stay with you."

"It's nice of—you," she says.

"Well," I say, "a lot of people say that I am overprotective. I don't know, I guess I know that you can wait alone, Melanie, but I figure *I* wouldn't like to wait alone . . ."

Melanie begins to hum: "Onward Christian Soldiers." I pick it up from her: anything to pass the time. Suddenly we are singing aloud. Suddenly we are having a marvelous time.

The last cab comes. Melanie jumps up to get into it, then turns back to me, the singing still all over her face, her lithe, fragile figure poised to step into the cab. "*I* didn't—see—that you were—overprotective, M-Mrs. Shepherd," she says. She reaches out and brushes my face with the tips of her fingers, delicately, delicately. "*I* saw—that you—were—kind—to us—" She pauses, thinks. "I—love you," she says, very clear, very decided. What other words does the prettiest girl need?

I am so touched. I am so touched. I feel shaken, fragile, young, answered by God.

I ride home on the next bus, humming "Onward Christian Soldiers" all the way. And singing it at the top of my voice when I get into the house.

Why do I stay, when they pay me peanuts? When they over-work me (all of us) to the point at which I could drop from weariness? When it all hurts so? Why, simple, Simon. I stay because the prettiest girl in Eau Claire touched my face with the gentlest touch anyone ever had. Because John calls me beautiful.

HOR-GHAY-LOO-EES-BOR-G-HAIS

I

This is going to be, I think, a long story and quite possibly a very boring one. If it is done exactly right—if that is I catch exactly the uncertain gleamings and shadow patterns that I seem to see at different levels in my thoughts—it is almost certain to be boring. But I have no real choice—I am compelled to write this story. The damn thing won't leave me alone. It keeps bugging me.

Whether it will turn out to be boring or interesting, though, is another question—I can't predict about that. The story will write itself as it chooses to be written. But I am immensely caught by the idea of it, and have been since Vange's birthday party, which was a month ago, in June.

There is another thing—I am afraid to write the story; I have been putting it off for weeks. What if I mess it up? It is so important to me. It is like the center of my life now: I have been thinking about it for so long, and so concentratedly. What will I do when I have written it? What shall I do when it is finished?

II

We were celebrating Vange's birthday (Peter and Vange and I) as we celebrated all of our birthdays this year, at the Orange Onion restaurant, which is down the street from the agency where we work. I don't remember what the original conversation was about—but I do remember that I stopped it cold.

"Peter—*Hor-ghay-loo-ees-borg-hais,*" I said.

"I knew you were going to say that," said Vange.

"What?" said Peter. He really said *vot,* because he has a Lithuanian accent, but I do not think it is important that I should try to reproduce Peter's accent. However, you might try to keep it in mind as he makes additional remarks here. Also, Vange (Evangeline Josephine, named for two dead aunts) and Peter are both blind, but that does not matter either. We work at an agency for blind people. That also does not matter, except insofar as I suppose that you want to know such details and will be annoyed with me if I do not give them to you. And if you are *too* annoyed, of course, you will not read my story.

But from the point of view of the story that has to be written, these details are absolutely irrelevant. That is, it seems to me at this moment that they are irrelevant.

"Horghay-looees-borghais," I said again to Peter, answering his "Vot?"

Vange laughed. Vange had been into this with me the whole day, and also the evening before. "This is Joan's new thing, Peter," she said. "Things take her this way—you remember the license plates?"

"Oh, god, I do remember the license plates," said Peter.

"Horghay-loo-ees-bor-ghays," I said, delighting in the sounds.

"But what *is* this Horhay?" asked Peter.

I spelled it out for him: J-O-R-G-E-L-U-I-S-B-O-R-G-E-S. "An Argentinean writer, Peter," I said. "A very great writer. You would like him very much, in fact you must read him, he is exactly your kind of writer."

Peter, as it turned out, did not know Borges—I have often thought that for really intelligent blind people, unless they have someone who will read to them whatever they want, one of the very great tragedies is that much of the world of literature is closed. The "Talking Book Service" folks tape many things, but of course they cannot tape everything, cannot possibly keep up with the millions and millions of words that are put into print every year, so they must of necessity aim what they do tape at a sort of average audience. Even fewer books are put into braille. So Peter, who is one of the most intelligent and potentially the most literate people I have ever known, has never read Borges.

Of course, if Borges is correct, or rather if my reading of Borges is correct, this should not matter. What matters is the mind that perceives—not the object of perception. The object can be anything—the questing mind creates the meaning, or unravels it—apprehends the whole of history and existence from a spool of thread. Or a starshot. Or a name.

"What was it that was said this morning about the new time for the staff meeting?" asked Peter, clearly trying to change the subject.

"Horghay-looees-borghais," I said. "Try it again. HOR-GG-HAY. LOO-EES. BOR-GHAIS."

"Horgay-looey-borkas," said Vange. "I'm really trying."

"I know you are, Vange, and I appreciate it," I said.

"You are boring!" said Peter. "You are both boring now."

I laughed at him. "I know, Peter," I said. "I'm sorry. Hor-ghay Loo-ees Borghais."

"How long am I going to have to put up with this?" Peter demanded.

"I don't know," I said. "It could be a long time. Horghay Looees Borghais."

Vange laughed. Peter groaned.

"You know, Vange, I woke up in the middle of the night, and I sat up in bed, and you know what I said?" I asked. "Out loud?" "Jorgay-Looish-Borka," said Vange.

"No, no," I said. "I said, 'Horghay-Looees-Borghais.'"

"Horghay-Looees-Borkas," said Vange.

"Good, Vange," I said. "You're getting it, I think."

Peter raised his hands toward heaven or the Orange Onion ceiling lantern in a gesture of supplication. "Oh, lord," he said. "What has happened to Joan? What is happening to Evangeline?"

"Poor Peter," said Vange, laughing at him.

"Yes, poor Peter," said Peter. "He hasn't got enough trouble in his life, his dear friends have got to give him more."

"It's Joan's *zahir*, Peter," Vange said kindly, confidentially.

I reached out and took Peter's hand and held it in both of my own hands. I focused on him as totally as I could. I looked into his sightless eyes, which are beautiful still, and which communicate humor and grace and intelligence. "HOR-G-HAY-LOO-EES-BORGHAIS, Peter," I said as carefully as I could. I was really trying. Can I help it if Peter is slower than Vange? Vange had got into it immediately the night before, was immediately into it with me.

Peter looked like he wanted to choke me.

But could *I* help it? Was it *my* fault?

III

The business about Borges began a long time before Vange's party. It was as though one reference was piled upon another until I finally had to take notice. And once I took notice, that was the end—I was done for, simply done for.

A few weeks before the party, a good friend of mine, Sarah Richardson, who is like me a social worker, telephoned. She asked me as a favor to her to read a story of Borges'—the one called "The Zahir." This was perhaps the fifth or sixth time that Borges was called to my attention and this was the time that was going to take hold. I am pretty intelligent, but I am very slow on the uptake; it sometimes takes a great deal of repetition to catch my attention and hold it.

Sarah wanted me to read this story because her brother-in-law in California, her sister's husband, has asked *her* to read it and to tell her what it meant, if she could. Sarah apparently is her brother-in-law's literary reference; as apparently I am hers. I have no literary reference person: I am the end of the chain. It is not that I think I am so terribly capable on this front; it is just that I once years ago placed my friend Elinor from Atlanta into this role, and she told me at that time that anyone who was so stupid that they could possibly ask what happened at the end of Henry James's *Portrait of a Lady* didn't deserve to know.

I learn hard, but I learn good. I have never again asked anyone what a work of literature means. Once burnt, twice shy, as the saying goes. I have decided that I am my own final reference; if I don't know myself what a thing means, then it has no meaning for me, and that's the end of it. It's not that I think I am so smart; it is simply that I have decided this, or accepted it—that if I don't know, then I don't deserve to know.

Perhaps it is pride; or on the other hand perhaps it is a form of common sense. Perhaps I do not want to be intellectually slugged again to no purpose; I still do not know what happened at the end of *Portrait of a Lady.*

The converse of this, however, is not true—I do not mind trying to explain meanings that I *do* grasp to others who solicit my elucidation. Generally speaking, though, I find that any attempt along these lines is nearly hopeless.

It may be simpler than I am making it sound; it may be as simple as this: that I am neither a good student nor a good teacher. That I am stuck into what I know by myself—capable neither of reception nor of transmission.

Whatever the case, I read "The Zahir" for Sarah. Well, you know that I loved it. I was simply knocked out by it. I understood something from it; I felt that I did. My head felt blown wide open by the cold, clean wind of comprehension. And what I understood would stay with me forever; I knew that.

Do you know that feeling?—that you have truly grasped something and made it yours, and because of it you can never be the same person you were before, you are utterly changed, and whether you want it or not, you can never go back, you can never *not* understand?

Once you have set your foot upon a certain path in this world, there is no turning back; the sole of your foot has taken an impress from that path, the path has become the sole of your foot, and wherever you set your foot down after that *is* the path. Like it or not, you are departed then upon a certain journey in this world, and to walk it to the end is inevitable.

In essence, "The Zahir" was a very simple story, contained a simple idea; but like most simple ideas, it was so strong and heavy that it had to be carried along by a stupendously complex assemblage of difficult words, sentences, and incidents. A man I knew in New York City once said something a long time ago: that if you had a really good new idea, you could shout it out in Times Square and no one would steal it. No one would *want* it; it would be too simple, it would sound obvious or stupid. So we write long and complex books and poems to carry simple ideas: to give the reader a chance to find out by himself, to give him a sense that he is a discoverer. Because, perhaps, what he does not himself discover, he will not believe? Or the belief, such as it is, will not be operative? Something like that. Perhaps.

Don't worry, I am not going to tell you what the Borges story means: I certainly do not want *you* to think that I am stupid. If you were to conclude at this point that I was stupid, obviously you would not read any more, and I want you to read some more, I am not anywhere near done with what I want to tell you. So I will not of course fall into the trap of trying to tell you what the story *means*. But it is easy, and I think relatively harmless, to tell you what the story is *about:* it is about a man (Borges himself) who becomes obsessed with a common Argentinean coin, which is a *zahir*. A zahir, in the terms of the story, is any absolutely irresistible obsessional object. There is extant at any one time in history only one zahir; but the zahir may be anything at different times. Borges feels that his obsession will become more and more total, until his Self, his separate identity, disappears into his compelled, unchosen contemplation of the coin. His conclusion is that behind the zahir, some time, after god knows what length of obsession, he may perhaps find God. He writes the story to tell us what is happening while he still can; since when the Self disappears—clearly—there will be no more possibility of telling any more stories; or at least not any more very good reasons for doing so.

I telephoned my friend Sarah—who turned this story loose upon me in what I assume was all innocence—and told her that I had read it.

"Did you understand it?" she said.

"Ah—no," I said.

"That's all?" she said. "Just—'no'?"

It did seem a little weak; I mean, a designated literary reference, once he or she has accepted the title, certainly has some obligation to take at least a shot at it.

"I don't think it was meant to be understood," I said. "I think that's the point of it. Sort of. Something like that. I mean, honestly, I think it *says* what it means."

"You are so goddamned exasperating sometimes," Sarah said.

"I know," I said. "I'm sorry."

"I'll never ask you for anything again," she said. "This is it."

"I don't blame you," I said. "I wouldn't ask me either."

The thing is, it wasn't that I didn't understand, or that I couldn't explain; it was that I wouldn't. I chose not to. I did not want to sound that stupid. There was also the possibility that I did not understand—that my understanding was simply wrong. I did not want to risk that. Deep down I am a really chicken person.

Then too (I rationalize to myself) there was the off chance that Sarah might not think I was stupid, that she might actually believe me, and I did not want to risk that either. I love my friend. These loose Truths and Meanings are dangerous stuff. You wouldn't ignite a stick of dynamite held in your hand unless you had pretty well accepted the idea that you didn't mind having your hand blown off. Would you?

IV

If you have—assuming that you are still with me, still reading; I told you right in the first paragraph that this would be boring if it was any good at all; you can't say I cheated you, I told you straight out, you have to admit it—if, as I said, you have some idea that if you hang in you will be rewarded, there will be a smashing ending to compensate for all this dithering, forget it. There will be no smash ending; such a result is simply inconceivable. This is a going-nowhere story. We are not going to get there. There is no place to go.

You want to hang in with me anyway? You think it is not possible that anyone would work this hard to write a story that has no point, no ending, no meaning? Well, I think you are wrong. But on the other hand, you could be right. How would I know, at this point? Maybe there *will* be an ending, a bang-up literary climax; why, a regular fireworks display! Maybe I'll blow my hands off. How will you know unless you hang in?

And if there isn't any ending, and you feel cheated by me, you can always crucify me. Stone me. Hang my heart from a weeping willow tree. Ride me out of Minneapolis, Minnesota, on a rail, tarred and feathered. Denounce me from the stage of the VFW bingo hall. Or call me stupid. Or crazy. Whatever is easiest for you.

V

I went over to Sarah's house a few days later; I said to her husband, Rick, who was there alone, Sarah and her two boys were off shopping, "Rick, you know that story Sarah wanted me to read?"

I wanted to check it out with Rick. Rick is, in his way, a person of unusually subtle intelligence; I wanted to sort of feel this out with him, grope around in his mind.

"What story?" he asked absently, concentrated on the case histories he was reading. Rick is a social worker too, and he is on the state parole board; he has to read, analyze, and make recommendations on hundreds of cases. You could say he plays a kind of God-role. He doesn't like it. He once tried to be a priest, but decided to be a social worker instead.

"'The Zahir,'" I said. "By Zhorzh Looey Borzhess."

That got him away from his cases all right.

"Zhorzh Looey Borzhess!" he shouted. "You don't by any chance mean Jorge Luis Borges, do you?"

I was charmed. "Say it again," I said.

"Horghay Looees Borghais," he said.

I tried to repeat it. Missed it. "Say it again," I demanded.

"Horghay Looees Borghais," he said.

"Again."

"Horghay Looees Borghais."

It took me a while, but I finally got it. It was the sound that fascinated me. I mean, the Om may grab some people, but Horghay Looees Borghais grabbed me that day.

I mean, I loved that name. I was taken by it. I had to get it
right.

"Is it really *Horr-ghhay,* Rick?" I asked. "Really that gargling
sound?"

"Well, the 'g' may be a little harder," he said. "Maybe a little
more like Hor-gay. In between somewhere."

I finally was satisfied. I finally figured I had it down cold. I
couldn't stop saying it. It wasn't a name any more; it was an in-
cantation. A person with an obsession may or may not be insane;
but one thing is certain: after a relatively short time, he is likely
to be an awful bore.

Horghay Looees Borghais.

VI

Vange is different. A psychiatrist (a previous administration decided that she needed one, and sent her to see one at the agency's
expense, an extraordinary measure for a business that in the first
place does not believe in psychiatry and that in the second place
is cheap beyond belief) once asked her if she thought she was
crazy, and she said she didn't think so, she thought she was different. Fine, the psychiatrist said, and that was that. (The adminis-
trator, let me tell you, was *so pissed* when he got the verdict. . . .)

Vange *is* different. I think I told you she was a social worker,
but actually she only works as a social worker; what she really is,
is a teacher, and she possesses lifetime teaching certificates in
two states. When she went to school—Vange is 61, so it was a
long time ago—few blind people were being accepted into cur-
ricula leading to teaching certificates. No one thought blind
people could teach; one of the excuses was that without eye contact they wouldn't be able to maintain discipline.

But Vange knows what she wants, and she gets it. She forced
her way (or, I imagine, quietly and firmly insisted her way) into a

program, got a teaching degree, and taught successfully for many years in public school systems in Minnesota and North Dakota. That was another thing Vange insisted upon—that she would not teach in segregated schools for blind people. At that time it was generally assumed that in the rare cases where blind people became teachers they would teach only other blind people.

Not our Vange. Vange says she does not see herself as a blind person: she sees herself as a person. Who happens to be blind.

The idea of Vange not being able to maintain discipline is comical. I have seen her pin our erratic director of services into his chair with a look—blind or not, the effect of her eye contact is devastating—and shut him up with a sentence: "Now then, Gregory Roger," she will say, "remember that I knew you when you were a pip-squeak . . ." Greg can't stand Vange. He also likes her very much. He depends heavily on her acute and intuitive intelligence in any critical situation.

We all feel this way about her in varying degrees: ambivalent. The degree of ambivalence depends upon the extent to which we can tolerate the sight of a human being self-actualizing right in front of our eyes.

Vange is more herself than anyone I know at the present time. And what is more, she keeps getting worse. She refuses to comb her hair, she looks like a round walking pincushion with a tangle of gray thread stuck on top of it. Her office is, you should excuse the in joke, a sight for sore eyes: piled high with junk. There is for example a plant sitting on top of a bookcase; this plant has been dead for at least two years. She says it is important to keep it: it is a reminder of the giver.

She sleeps in her swivel chair, little catnaps, leaning back at a terrifying angle.

Greg gets very mad at her about these naps; he says to me: "It looks awful, I am ashamed to take board members past her door."

I say: "You could solve the problem in ten minutes by putting a curtain over her door window."

Greg: "But you are her supervisor! Tell her not to do it!"

Me: "Greg—it doesn't matter to me. It doesn't matter to me that she sleeps. She rehabilitated a guy with a goddamn frontal lobotomy once. What do I care that she sleeps? What do I care that she doesn't look good?"

It is only because Vange is working there that I am not the irritating self-actualizer in the agency. I'm pretty good at it, and getting better; only when I am compared to Vange do I look like a piker. Compared to Vange, I am well groomed, satisfactorily dressed, neat, efficient, cooperative, and quiet. Also, I do not sleep in my chair. When God wants me to sleep in my chair, I will, I tell myself. Vange makes me feel guilty about it, though. Vange is a horror.

"Am I obnoxious?" she asks me.

"Yes," I say.

"Do *you* find me obnoxious?" she asks.

"Yes, Vange, extremely," I say. We have been over this many times. It is a joke. It is not a joke. I do find Vange obnoxious. I probably want to punch her out as much as Greg does. I also like her. It is possible that I love her.

Vange is right into the zahir thing with me. She really wants to pronounce Jorge Luis Borges the way I do; but she can't. She does not have an ear for the pronunciation of language.

She tries and tries.

Jorghghkky Looie Borkass.

My god.

*Hor*ghghkky-Loo-ass-Borg-g-g-as.

Tch.

No. Not right, Vange.

She has at last come up with her own formulation. She has given up on what I say is the right way.

Gorgeous Louie Borgia.

VII

These self-actualizers are terribly dangerous people. They upset everybody's applecart. They threaten everything we believe about ourselves. Think about it. Civilization is based on people being predictably like one another.

You want to see a Kafka sight?—have a real hallucinatory experience? Stand on any busy street corner. Watch the people going across the street when the light turns green. A predictable, trained mass. For that moment, not a person in the crowd. Sad. Horrifying. Terrible. If you see it at a certain wry angle. Necessary. Admirable.

I mentioned this about the green light to Vange. She agreed. I said, "You go across with the green lights, though, Vange. Like everybody else."

"Of course," she said. "What do you think I am? Crazy?"

VIII

Vange has begun to muse and meditate about the zahir, and to phone me about it at odd times.

"I have decided," she says, "that my old tennis shoes are my zahir."

"Yeah?" I say.

"Maybe my hair is my zahir," she says another time. I am getting a little tired of this.

Horrg-hay Loo-ees Borg-ghais. The right way is the right way. Plain as the nose on your face. Plain as the rolling-around eyes in Vange's head. Nystagmus, she has. Nystagmus—now there's another good word for you: heavens, it can be anything.

"Maybe my messy desk is my zahir," she says. "Maybe your messy desk is just a goddamned nuisance, Vange," I say. "A goddamned rebellion."

"So?" she says. "What's the difference between a rebellion and a zahir?"

"A rebellion you are in control of," I say.

"You better believe it," says Vange.

In my secret heart I do not think that Vange is quite getting it. Rational Peter is meanwhile hanging in with both of us. Laughing at us; delighting in us. Perhaps we are his projections; perhaps the madness in Peter is us.

Horgghay Looees Borgghais.

IX

I feel that in a way I promised to tell you about the license plates. (You say you are tired of this? You say you don't *want* to hear about the license plates? Tough. Try not getting the license plates; they will find you wherever you are. *This is a threat.*) (Don't you want to see me blow my hands off? *Oh, please stay. Please.*)

One day about three years ago I was driving over to Sarah's house—you remember Sarah, of Sarah-and-Rick?—on the other side of town from where I live. I had a canvas purse on the car seat beside me.

As I pulled up to a red light behind another car I absently noted that the license plate on the car ahead of me said Montana. Several blocks later, in the same situation, stopped at a red light, I saw a Mississippi license plate on the car ahead. *Wow, Mississippi,* I said to myself: that can't be a real common license plate around here. (This is Minnesota, the only place closer to the edge of the world is the Northwest Territories.)

Then—would you believe it? my *god*—I saw a Northwest Territories license plate. I couldn't believe it. *Northwest Territories!* I mean, Jesus.

By the time I got to Sarah's house I had seen also Nebraska and Wyoming, as well as the obvious ones, Minnesota, Iowa,

North Dakota. I thought, I don't want to forget them, there is something about this that is fun. I can add some more on the way home. For the fun of it. But my memory is so bad; I'll forget. Then the great idea came: I'll take a ballpoint pen and write the names of the ones I've seen on my canvas purse. That will be the point: to see them and mark them down on my purse. This will be my license plate purse.

That was the beginning of the whole license plate thing. I got more and more into it. I marked ordinary license plates in black; unusual ones in red. When I saw seconds and thirds of plates I had seen already, I noted them by drawing little flowers after the original printing of the place name. I knew it was screwy. But I was having such a good time. Every ride across town was a wonderful adventure.

The people from the Agency caught it from me; at first they thought it was a little strange, but then they saw the fun in it. Everett, who is the supervisor of the rehabilitation center, confessed his terrible secret—that he collected matchbook covers. Andrea in Personal and Home Management came in one day and made a special point of finding me: "Joan," she said excitedly, "listen, there's a car parked on Twenty-sixth and Lyndale with a Puerto Rico license plate. . . ."

I couldn't go and see it; I had an interview first thing that morning, and after that the whole day turned into chaos and I couldn't go and see it. Obviously you have to draw the line somewhere. I still don't have Puerto Rico. I regret this.

But I do have Guam, and Hawaii, and Alaska.

Most of the Canadian provinces.

All but one of the fifty states.

And would you believe *Prince Edward Island?*

Rhode Island I have not got. For a while I wanted Rhode Island more than anything.

But the fever is over now. A shining is gone from my life. A drive across town is now just a drive across town. It is no longer an adventure.

I can't get it back; I'm just not interested anymore. However, if I should one day happen to see Rhode Island . . . maybe then . . .

I was nuts. El nutso. I knew it. But I was having such a lot of fun. And it did seem innocent. It did not seem as though anything about my collecting license plates could hurt anything or anybody. Except that perhaps the sight of an otherwise sane and normal person entirely captivated by a crazy and useless project is dangerous? To the moral fabric, perhaps?

Golf is ok. Jogging is ok. War is ok. Collecting license plates when you are a 48-year-old social worker is not ok. I can understand this. Honestly, I can.

An unfortunate thing did happen in connection with collecting license plates; I will tell you more about this later. I mean, I think I had better save it. I am getting a little nervous about the ending of this story, maybe I could throw that thing in at the end in case nothing else turns up that looks like it might be taken for an ending. Remember a name—Amanda.

X

Well, I've changed my mind: I'll tell you part of it now instead of later. Amanda's husband is John Harris, John Robinson Harris, and you could say that John got me started on Jorge Luis Borges in the first place. John was the first one who mentioned Borges to me. John was at that time an associate professor in the English Department at Macalester College in St. Paul, and he was teaching Borges in a class. One day he said to me, you could write stories a lot like Jorge Luis Borges if you wanted to. When I told him that I had never heard of Borges, he made me sit down and read "The Circular Ruins" on the spot. I did like it. He also recommended "The Three Versions of Judas" and a story about

Don Quixote. He told me the title of a book to buy: *Labyrinths.*

But I was not into writing at that time. Besides, I did not want to do anything at all "like" anybody else. I forgot about it, pretty much. The pronunciation of the name did not strike me then. It all stayed in the back of my mind, though; it surfaced every once in a while: hey, you, you could write like what's-his-name. John Robinson Harris says so.

Months later I got on a bus one morning. Sat next to a young boy. Who was reading *Labyrinths.* Ok, I said to myself. Enough. I will get a copy of *Labyrinths.* Uncle.

It took me another couple of months to get the book. When I had it, I sat down and reread "The Circular Ruins." And then read also "Three Versions of Judas." And the story about the man who rewrote the *Don Quixote,* and in which the second version was exactly like the first, word for word, but was considered critically to have gained something, was considered better than the first version. Why, isn't that a marvelous idea? Isn't that absolutely a grabber? Isn't that just wonderfully crazy? Why, also, isn't that playful? Isn't it *innocent?*

The day after I started reading the book I got on a bus and sat next to a woman who was holding on her lap the same book. The signs do mount up. Surely you have noticed that. Sooner or later it takes a really deliberate decision to avoid them.

"Too fucking *much,*" I said to myself. To the woman, who was middle-aged, well dressed, and rather on the plump side, I said: "Interesting stories, aren't they?"

"Oh, yes," she said. "Have you read them all?"

"Well," I said. "Some of them."

She: "Have you read 'The Circular Ruins'?"

Me: "Yes, I did read that one."

She: "Did you understand it? I am reading it for a class I'm taking, and none of us understands it. Do you?"

There it was. "No," I said. "Not understand exactly. But I

don't feel that I have to understand it. I don't feel that that's the point. I feel that I can just sort of *have* it."

I could see the wheels turning in her head, it was wonderful to watch. She got something. She liked what she got.

"I think I . . . *see,*" she said softly. "Is it like a mystical experience? You don't have to understand it? You can just *have it?*"

"Sort of like that," I said. "Something like that. That's what I think anyway."

"Thank you," she said. "Really—I mean it. Thank you very much." She turned away from me, back, into herself. She smiled to herself. "You don't *have to understand* . . ." she murmured.

I got off the bus at my stop by the agency. The agency is for blind people. I guess I told you that before. But maybe you didn't remember.

It was just about here in the sequence that Sarah asked me to read "The Zahir"; and that I did read it for her.

But surely John Harris is wrong; I cannot write like Jorge Luis Borges. Surely Borges is above all else an intensely intellectual and erudite writer. I am just not smart enough. All those tangled, studded paragraphs, crammed with esoteric information; all those footnotes documenting dusty corners of libraries, the years of study, the mastery of odd information of all kinds, strange, occult, or familiar as today—I could never write like Borges. I would have to become a scholar to do it, and I just don't have it in me.

On the other hand, I am, you know, *smart* enough. Actually, I am *very* smart. I just don't happen to have a passion for study at the present time. But who knows what may happen to me tomorrow, who knows what I may become tomorrow?

They say that Jorge Luis Borges was blind before he died.

XI

I have only one more incident to tell you about. (Oh, come on, you can stand still for *one more incident,* can't you? I mean, you've come *this far?* Don't you want to see me blow my hands off?)

As part of my job at the agency, I went to a party for senior citizens at the Huntington Park Recreation Center. When I got there I went into my social worker act—I walked around, introducing myself to people, being warm, open, friendly, and outgoing. In my real life, I am a shy person; most of the time I would be afraid to behave in such a way in my real life.

I met another social worker there who was helping to run the show. She talked about an Argentinean couple who were coming to the party later. She said the man spoke no English at all, and his wife not much more. She was worried about them, concerned that they would feel strange. She had a student with her who spoke a little Spanish; this young woman was going to take a shot at serving as an interpreter.

The couple came: a man of maybe 65, and a woman perhaps a few years younger. The man was very handsome, very attractive, a marvelous face, why, a movie star face, aquiline nose, thick waves of white hair carefully combed back. The woman was distinguished, vivid, vital. They were absolutely out of it, they were relating to nobody.

I sat down with them at a table with the social worker and the interpreter, who were attempting small talk. Got myself introduced. Said—"I was reading one of your great Argentinean writers yesterday." The interpreter translated.

"Oh?" came the translation back. "Which writer?"

"Hor-ghay Looees Bor-ghais," I said.

Why, they got it without any translation. I was so pleased with myself.

"Oh!—*Borges!*" they said in unison.

Well, you know I was in like Flynn. But the rest of it had to be translated. Dumb luck will take you only just so far.

Borges is a wonderful old man, he should have got the Nobel Prize. I couldn't agree with you more, I think you're absolutely right. *He is considered a very noble man, in Argentina, a wise man, a very noble old man, do you know "noble"?—very respected.* The translation was halting and slow and probably inaccurate. We all understood each other perfectly. Or so it seemed to me.

The whole story came. Of a man and a woman, Jews, in the last terrible days of World War II. Of emigration after the war to Argentina. Of their only son, born in Argentina, moved to the USA. Of their tearing up their roots once again, after all this time, to come to Minnesota—the edge of the world—to spend the last years of their lives where their son was.

I told them about my ex-husband, an American soldier nineteen years old, in Czechoslovakia during the last three months of the war. The things that happened to him, that he could never forget, that changed him forever.

The woman said finally, and the translator repeated: "Enough. Enough. We have remembered the bad days. Now we will pay attention to the fact that we are at a nice party . . ."

Why, I loved them. I loved them. We embraced all around. Kissed. Over and over. Ate cake. Watched the senior citizens.

XII

Now we need the windup, right? I mean, I promised you only one last incident, I do keep my promises. But there has to be an ending. The ending comes after the last incident. I did not cheat you. I did not lie to you. Not yet, anyway.

Remember Amanda? I told you to remember that name? She won't talk to me anymore. Amanda loved me, I know she did, I know she was a true friend. And I don't entirely know why she has cut me out of her life—"dropped me," as they say. But I do know one thing that happened. It was about the license plates; she was startled when I first brought up the idea, but then she was enchanted by it. She drove me around two college campuses, one summer afternoon, looking for license plates. She explained to her two daughters, ages five and eleven, that Auntie Joan was into license plates. When I think of some of the cockeyed and wonderful activities that Amanda Harris has at various times drawn me into, I know that license plate hunting was ok with her. Amanda was absolutely one of my favorite people of all time. And for sure license plate hunting was ok with her.

But then I told her husband John—John Robinson Harris, you remember *him*—what I generalized from the license plate thing: John, I said, I understand at last what happiness is. It is finding a thing you really like to do, *and doing it.* Even if it is some wacky thing like building little houses out of toothpicks, something utterly dumb like that.

Amanda said afterwards, for god's sake don't say things like that to John. He wants to become a gardener. He wants to drop out. He has responsibilities. *He can't become a gardener.* He can't drop out. Don't give him these ideas of yours.

At a certain point, not long after that, Amanda decided (apparently) that she didn't need me in her life.

With Rick and Sarah, I have been a little more sensible. Rick has just resigned from the parole board. He served on it and hated it for six years. He was an idealist; he thought he could in some way be of some great service, find some way to change the way things were. Social worker, priest, what difference is there? Neither is concerned any more with immortal things.

He wanted all his life to get on the parole board. He got what he wanted. And decided that there is such a thing as evil, and that some people want to be that thing, cannot be talked, therapized, or rehabilitated out of it. It has destroyed him, this decision. He wants to take a year off, do nothing, rest, bum, write, recover. He cannot recover, but maybe he can find a balance, make some kind of peace.

Sarah does not want him to do this, she wants him to get another job. She has two young sons to raise, to send to college. Is she wrong?

She is not wrong. Of course not.

I am silent. Well, reasonably silent. Silent for me. I certainly do not want to lose another friend. With Amanda gone there aren't that many left.

Vange says, "I think you and I do not really have the same idea of what the zahir is."

I agree with her. We do not. No one controls the zahir. Obviously. By definition. I do not think I will push it. It would be pretty hard to turn Vange off of me, but I think it could be done.

Peter meets me in the hall at the agency. "How is Hor-hay?" he asks. "Fine," I say: "I am writing a story about Hor-hay." He laughs, pleased with his vicarious participation in a lunacy he will not share.

"You are cr-r-r-azy, Joan," he says. And smiles at me.

When I bring in a really exciting matchbook cover to Everett one day, he tells me that he is sorry he has given me the impression that he collects the matchbook covers for himself, actually he collects them for his young son, Stephen, eleven years old. I don't believe this. But I say nothing.

I have a fantasy: in it someone figures out what Jorge Luis Borges is saying, what he means. No noble old man, he, but a saboteur; a sly fox, one who plants doubts, one who sows awful seeds. In darkness, in secret, in heavy, studded, weighted, hidden paragraphs, he tells his truth. They find him out. They tar and feather him and ride him out of Argentina on a rail, 82 years old (or whatever) and blind. *Noble old man?*—not he!—young, rather; seeing visions; star-gazed, amazed; a crazy child playing. No Nobel Prize for him; a cross, maybe. A weeping willow tree.

It will not happen, though. His disguise is perfect; he is disguised as a writer.

(Actually, you know, he is dead now: an even more convincing mask.)

I have read recently a critical essay on Borges. It seems that he made up a lot of his parenthetical references, his erudite footnotes. It seems that he knew a lot, but invented whatever he did not know. Clever—oh, clever! I am filled with admiration.

They also say that Borges was not always a writer of stories. He was a poet before that. One day he incurred a terrible head injury, fell on his head or something like that, and after that he was a story writer. (This is true. Would I make up a thing like this? Anything at all can happen, obviously. Over the edge of the world are wondrous possibilities.)

Did you see me blow my hands off?

WILMA BREMER'S FUNERAL

There are so many deaths here, that's the main thing you have to grasp right at the start. It isn't that we get used to it, ever, or that we don't care. We do care. I have cried over all the ones who died, or most of them, and got drunk over a few. We all get drunk over a few. And sometimes we rage and scream and curse God. We have been known to pray.

So we are not hardened to the fact of death; it is more like we get confused: *Which is life and which is death? Who is alive and who is dead?*

Deaths seem to come in threes: we wait for the second, and the third, always. We are a superstitious crew, as well as being odd in a number of other respects.

We are called upon to feel so much. The mind rebels. Refuses for a while. Will grieve tomorrow.

And for what should we grieve? For young life, or old, cut off in the midst of what awful pain? What enormity of despair? Better grieve for the birth of the child, better grieve life than death. But we are just ordinary teachers and social workers and nurses, we take it in the only way we know how—we grieve, when we have the time, the luxury, for the loss of our friends, whom we knew better than we knew our husbands and wives and children, because they were in pain, and they told us about it, shared pain, that bitter bread, more nourishing than any other.

Tomorrow's grief never comes. By tomorrow we have something else to worry about. Bruce's doctor says that Bruce has an inoperable tumor of the brain; Bruce (who is in the sheltered workshop) is both deaf and blind; how will we tell him, how will we make him understand that soon he will not be able to work at all anymore? Work here is his whole life.

Sharon dies. She was (we have heard) very depressed for about a month before she died. She wanted to talk to us—we got that message. We did not call; we are on some level intolerably ashamed that we did not call.

We loved Sharon, and we did a good job for her. She said she could not possibly bear to live and be blind; she sobbed through the whole intake interview. I was the intake worker then, I did the interview—what a word for such an event: initiation, consecratory rite, invitation to Pinocchio's Pleasure Island, to the Good Ship Lollipop; but *interview?*—I put my arms around her, I made her smile; her smile was a marvelous gift to me. I promised her that if she came to us, we could make her feel better in a month. But it took us only a week. We are very, very good at the job we do here in the rehabilitation center. By the time Sharon left us, five months later, she hummed and sang all day long; we always knew where Sharon was because we could hear her singing. And those of us who can see (are not blind, that is) could spot her jaunty sunshade hat, bobbing happily along on top of fat, short Sharon, indoors or out.

I guess you could say Sharon was a character, one of our favorites. "You really are something else, Sharon," I said to her once. "Like what else?" she said. "A three-legged horse?" "Like something wonderful, like a unicorn," I said. Every once in a while one of them gets to us just a little more than the others—it isn't fair, but there it is.

Eighteen months later Sharon is dead, of diabetes, gangrene, and finally kidney failure. She was just my age, which is forty-seven. I identify with her—this is a mortal sin in my business. She was happily married, which I am not. She had a hundred good reasons for living. I am hard pressed to list three for myself, unless I list my friends as one reason each. Six of us went to the funeral. I did not go. I came down with flu instead.

There are just too many deaths.

II

Who is this "we," "us," I am talking about? Well, there's me, the author of this story. I am the manager of community services at the Center for the Blind. Up to a couple of months ago I did intake, which is how it happened that I did the intake on Sharon Wald, who was happy for seventeen months because of what we did, depressed for one month, and now is dead. Then there is another social worker, Vange Kuhlman—you have heard about her before in these stories—she is the best and bravest and smartest of us all. Vange is partially sighted because of a birth defect, sixty-one years old now, fat and cheerful. But even she, who (asked) is always "most excellent!", has her moments of crap-out.

Then there are the teachers in the rehabilitation center, who teach blind people how to walk with white canes, for example (that is a terrifying job, I don't know how the hell they can do it; most of the mobility instructors are—or become—very different from the rest of us, somewhat withdrawn and apart. And they more or less consider themselves the high priests of our remark-able craft, as strange and esoteric and religious in its way as any ancient Egyptian embalmer's trade); other teachers who teach blind people how to read braille, use an abacus; how to cook without burning themselves and everything else up when they can't see the fire; how to type, write checks, use cassette recorders, how to knit, model in clay, crochet, weave, do macrame, play poker, and use the power saw. (You think I am putting you on, I'm not, we do teach blind people to use power tools, why not? We've even got a blind hockey team, blind archers.)

And there are others of us who teach blind people how to work, do jobs, earn money, support themselves and their families, view themselves as workers—after all, that's where it's at, isn't it? You earn money, you are worth something? You do not, you aren't?

So we teach blind people to work.

III

I promise I'll get to Wilma's funeral quite soon now; I have to lead up to it like this because if I don't you won't have the background, you will maybe think it was just awful, grotesque, and it wasn't, it was really nice, like Gerald said it was. I am coming to Gerald soon too—he is another important person in this story. In fact, I have only a few more preliminary remarks. Put up with me, please? I give you my word it is going to be worth it. Listen, have I ever lied to you?—trust me: I say that to all my clients—it seems to me that you are in a way at this moment a client of mine.

So anyway, we teach blind people to work. Some of them go into our sheltered workshop more or less permanently; some of them use the shop as a transitional experience and go on to work in "The Community." "The Community" is you, assuming you are free, whatever that means, not necessarily white, any age between eighteen and seventy, and possessed of whatever wit, dexterity, skill, mental ability, education, and degree of health are necessary to earn an adequate paycheck in the competitive job market.

Some of the blind people, though, stay in the sheltered workshop more or less forever; for whatever reason, mental or physical, they cannot hack it in the fierce, competitive, unloving, no-quarter arena where you and I earn our livings.

IV

One of the people in the sheltered workshop is Gerald. Gerald is totally blind and spent thirty years of his life in a state mental hospital—years ago they put many, many blind children in state hospitals as "untrainable." Evangeline Kuhlman got Gerald out, worked with him as his counselor for maybe a year, and now he is in the shop. Vange taught him (what a remarkable accomplishment, think about it) to like himself. Gerald has many of what we call in the trade "blindisms": he rocks, rubs his hands together, pokes his fingers into his eyes. Other things, some too obscene to mention, but funny, interesting, human: alive. He is not retarded, not at all—but he is very different from you and me: he is kind, considerate, loving and warm, and he knows absolutely that he is a good and worthwhile person. I do not believe he is capable of deliberate cruelty—at least, I have never seen that capacity in him, I suppose he has it, he is after all as human as you or me. But his thinking is different from yours and mine—it is right to the point.

He is, I suppose you could say, damaged beyond any hope of further repair by those thirty years in a state hospital and by being born blind; that is, he will never look like you or me. He will never work in "The Community."

He calls Vange and me "his two lovely ladies." I am honored to be included, I do not really deserve it, but this is Gerald's great courtesy. He calls all the women he talks to "hon." He buys roses and gives them away sometimes on the bus on his way home to his apartment downtown. He calls up Social Security once in a while when some problem arises. I have heard some of these conversations:

Gerald: "Hello, hon, I just called, um, called to ask you about the NOTICE I have received . . ."

Phone: "Blup, blup, blup . . ."

Gerald: (Pausing, obviously considering how to do this kindly) ". . . well, yes, hon, I do hear what you are saying. And— hon—I wouldn't want to put you down or anything—*oh, I wouldn't do that for worlds—you know that*—but, hon, if it's all right with you I think I'll just check this out with Mrs. Kuhlman and see what she has to say."

Phone: "Blup, blup, BLUP . . ."

Gerald: "Oh, hon, I don't want to hurt your feelings, really and truly I don't. I know you do the best you can. But you see the fact of the matter is Mrs. Kuhlman, um, knows more about Social Security than you do."

Phone: "Blup."

They thoroughly dislike Mrs. Kuhlman at Social Security, because Gerald is right, she does know more about it than they do. Why shouldn't she, she is certainly some kind of genius, and it certainly takes a genius to understand Social Security.

Gerald said: "Oh, I'm *glad* you see it that way, I'll just talk to Mrs. Kuhlman then, you know she and I have been friends for many many years, and then I'll call you back."

Phone said: "Blup, blup."

Gerald: "Goodbye then, and I do thank you, hon, you've been very helpful to me . . ." There is a long pause, Gerald is thinking how to end this with real grace, apparently: "Hon, it isn't that I question your intelligence and goodwill, it is just that I think a person should get many different opinions in a matter of this, um, *consequence.* 'DON'T YOU?" Who could argue?

I had a dream a couple of nights ago: I dreamed that our building had been knocked down into bricks and all the bricks and chairs and desks and everything had been auctioned off and after it was all over, the total assets, when all the bills had been paid, amounted to $138. I mean, what good is $138 in the face of our task? We were finished—God knows this is not far from the truth. And Vange Kuhlman was sitting amid all the leftover rubble and she was crying. "Oh, what will happen to the people in the workshop?" she was crying.

V

Wilma Bremer was also one of the people in the workshop. But she was one of the ones who could see. Some of the people in the shop (never over thirty percent) have to be sighted; there are some parts of certain operations—and how we hate to admit it, but we do try to be a little realistic here; although realism is not our long suit, hope is more like it, denial is more like it—there are some things that do require sight. There are some things that blind people can't do: brain surgery, flying a plane, and certain tricky operations in the workshop. Wilma was a line supervisor in the shop. That was all I knew about her—I mean, that is all the information that I connected with her name.

You have to understand that there is a great chasm, a barrier, between "Rehab" and "The Shop," so that very few of the people from the shop know the people from rehab, and vice versa. Essentially, I think rehab is shy and aloof because they are somehow afraid of the workshop. And the workshop is very resentful of what they perceive as rehab's disdainful attitude toward them.

Rehab is the class operation—the showpiece of the agency—it is clean, righteous, haloed, the people in it seem to think of themselves as somehow better. (Confess—in your deepest heart, don't *you* think *you* are better than a worker on a factory assembly line?) The workshop is like any other factory—the people who work in it get dirty, greasy, covered with lint, etc. The workshop nurses a terrible anger against rehab; whenever anything goes wrong, especially financially, it is "rehab's fault." And it is, too—rehab is expensive, it is the son or daughter going to college, it cannot support itself entirely. The workshop is the old mother and father who toil and drudge to support that glittering child—but sometimes they are hurt and angry even when they are proud. Especially if that child won't speak to them, especially if he (or she) seems to be ashamed of them.

Rehab is ashamed of its hardworking parent: the workshop. It is a very uneasy relationship. Apparently it cannot be resolved. So the people in rehab do not know many of the people in the workshop.

There is another thing to be considered—the agency is large, there are just too many people to know them all. And the faces keep changing. And rehab is intense, concentrated upon its difficult task.

Vange, though—an exception to every rule I know—knows everybody, loves everybody. She also remembers everybody. She is becoming a sort of legend here: the phone will ring in her office and a voice will say, Hi, Vange, remember me? and she will say, I remember your voice, talk some more and your name will come to me, and the person talks some more and by god! from twenty years back the name comes to her. The person on the phone is terribly pleased, of course: but how does she do it? She says it is a matter of paying attention to people all the time, of knowing every minute that each one of them is totally and individually important.

At the very end of this story, I am going to tell you some more about this; don't forget, or at the end you will think my story has no point. *Don't forget. Pay attention.* (I do know how hard it is; I am like you, I have not learned the trick.)

VI

One Monday morning I arrived at the agency and Vange told me that Wilma Bremer had died suddenly of a heart attack over the weekend, and her funeral was to be Tuesday morning. A lot of the people from the shop wanted to go to the funeral and there weren't enough sighted guides. Would I go as a sighted guide?

"Sure, Vange," I said. It meant no more than that to me, you see, Sure, Vange, we have an emergency situation and everybody (well, all the good folks anyway) pitches in and helps out, part of the job, part of the day's work. I didn't know Wilma Bremer from Adam.

As usual, "not enough sighted guides" turned out to be an understatement. I drove four people over to the church in my car; presumably I was to be their sighted guide too. I think there was Bob Troy and Louisa, both total (totally blind, that is), Rene (total), and maybe one partial (partially sighted, anything from 20/200 visual acuity to bare light perception) but I don't remember anymore who it was. I don't even remember for sure that it was Rene and Bob and Lou, I didn't really know them at the time, I have got to get this across to you, I was just an instrument in this situation. I was just doing my job.

I also wanted to go because Evangeline, though she is true blue and goes to all of them, really gets upset by funerals. I wanted to be with her. I mean: I knew Vange.

VII

Now, there is a prescribed technique for sighted guide. There is one sighted guide and one blind person. The blind person holds the arm of the sighted person just above the elbow, four fingers in towards the guide's body, thumb out; the blind person walks half a step behind the sighted person, who then leads easily and gracefully and in a way that is perfectly dignified and inconspicuous. There are subtle signals: a slight hesitation before a flight of stairs, for example. A signal meaning: follow behind me single file, we are going through a narrow space.

There are good reasons for every detail of this technique, but this is a story, you don't have to get all of it, for god's sake, if you hold out for all of it we'll never make it to the funeral. I only want you to have enough so that you can understand.

Sighted guide becomes automatic after you've done it a few thousand times. It is a very beautiful thing to see when it is done properly; and it is a very beautiful thing to experience. It is an act of pure service, economical, absolutely appropriate, not too much given, not too little. The blind person (if he's a good sort—there are a few holdouts in any category) receives it as such, and this receiving, acceptance, on his or her part, makes it an interaction, a gift, perfectly offered, perfectly received. How many gifts are that pure? I absolutely love being a sighted guide.

Touch comes into it too: the act of serving as sighted guide is, in this culture in which touch is pretty much forbidden, a sanctioned and permitted way to touch another human being physically. If a blind person comes to us afraid to touch people, we must try to break down that fear. We order up The Treatment: touch, touch, touch. And love. You never saw a place where people hug each other, touch each other, so much.

And when the guide leads his or her own friends, other signals develop. Peter (Lithuanian, blinded in World War II and our communication skills instructor) is my friend. I squeeze Peter's hand between my arm and my body when I lead him—this means: I love you, Peter, we are friends. Peter grips my arm a little tighter—this means, I love you too, Joan, I agree with you that we are friends. When I lead Vange, on the rare occasions when she may need it, the message is more complex: it is, maybe you need this and maybe you don't, but for the sake of seven years' affection let us pretend that you need it, humor me, dammit, you stubborn old woman, if you trip and fall I will feel bad. So humor me. Love me. Accept from me a gift you do not want.

VIII

But believe me, none of the subtle stuff, none of this beautiful sighted guide technique, went on at Wilma Bremer's funeral. It was bedlam, it was a real hash out in the lobby or whatever you call that entry part of a church. I can't remember exactly, but I imagine that I took two people in first, one on each arm, and then asked them to wait for me while I went back for the other two.

I do remember saying to someone, "Now stand right here, don't move until I get back . . ." But they didn't stand there of course—why should they? This was the funeral of one of their own, they did as they damn pleased, as indeed they should. Up to a point. I mean, tripping or poking people with the white cane is strictly out, as is stepping on toes or crashing into people. A certain amount of this is however unavoidable in a crowd situation, unless you've got one-to-one on sighted guide, which somehow never seems to happen in the clutch.

When I got back, the two I had left were gone, someone else had taken them into the church, and I ended up with Gerald Lennox. Vange took Jenny Mattson who is very hard of hearing as well as blind.

I led Gerald into the church and we found a far forward pew with Vange and Jenny. We hadn't sat there a minute when Gerald said: "Can we go right up to the casket, Joan? To pay our respects?"

"Certainly we can, Gerald," I said. So we got out of the pew and joined the line of mourners going up to review the open casket. Vange and Jenny followed us.

When it was our turn, Gerald said, "Can we go right up to it, Joan?" It was dumb of me not to know that he wanted that, of course, how else could he see it, but to touch it?

The truth is, I was scared. I knew what was coming, and I can take a lot, but the idea of what he had in mind was embarrassing to me. I mean, Christ, who touches a casket, who feels a corpse? A blind person who really cares about the person in the casket, that's who. I admit it, and I am ashamed of it—Gerald was going to be an embarrassment to me.

I led Gerald right up so that his body touched the casket—good sighted guide technique there, recommended by AFB, which is the American Foundation for the Blind: "Lead the person to the chair so that he can feel it with his body . . ." Gerald reached his hand out and found the satin fabric, very delicately brushed it, rubbed it.

"Satin!" he said.

"What color is it," he said. Sighed.

"Kind of peach-colored, Gerald," I told him. Very cool, I was.

"Peach-colored!" he said. "Isn't that nice? Isn't that nice for Wilma, Joan? She was a wonderful, wonderful person, Joan—did you know her?"

"Well, no, I didn't, Gerald," I said.

Gerald: "And are there flowers in the casket, Joan?" I looked at the roughened, folded hands, hands of a worker, resting at last, lying crossed on exquisite pink and white carnations.

"Yes, Gerald, she is holding a really nice bouquet of pink and white carnations."

"Oh!" said Gerald. "Pink and white carnations!" When Gerald gets really excited, he lowers his voice to a level of truly dreadful lugubrious enthusiasm. "Isn't that nice. Isn't that *wonderful.* She will be missed, Joan," he sighed, sobbed, breathed. *"Yes, she will be missed . . ."*

Then—"Um, Joan, would it be asking too much if I could,

um, *touch the flowers?*"

"No, it wouldn't be asking too much, Gerald," I said.

Very cool lady here. Fuck them all, I thought, these sighted outsiders, relatives and priests and what have you, who will think Gerald is inappropriate. Fuck appropriate.

I guided Gerald's hand to the flowers. *("Guide* the blind person's hand to the object . . ." I could hear the AFB movie tape playing in my head.) He touched them with one finger, brushed them, caressed them, as delicately, as gently, as surely, as I imagine an artist would touch an original Rembrandt.

Eventually, of course, he touched her hand. "Oh—that's-her-hand-isn't-it-Joan? That's-Wilma's-hand," he breathed, terribly excited.

"Yes, Gerald," I said. "That's her hand."

"Cold in death," he said. Tears started to his eyes.

"Yes, cold in death . . ." He squeezed Wilma's hand, pressed it again and again, hard, for a long time.

I would like to tell you that I looked calmly around and saw the church so that I could describe for you now what it looked like. As a matter of fact I would like to stick something in here for what writers call "pace"—every trade has its tricks—but the truth is I can't remember a thing. I was absolutely focused and fixed upon Gerald's hand and Wilma's. I could hear my mother's voice in my ear from a long time ago: *What will the neighbors think?*

And behind me, as if from another country, far away, I registered as background a strange discreet roaring whisper, which was Vange trying to tell Jenny what was going on: GERALD IS HOLDING WILMA'S HAND, JENNY. But in a whisper, pitched just right, it is possible they heard it outside in the street. Vange doesn't worry about the neighbors, nor for the most part about anything else; supervising Vange has its trials at times.

"Joan, what does she look like?" Gerald asked. "I mean, her face for example, and have they done her hair nicely for her?"

I looked for the first time at the permed, marcelled head resting on the peach satin pillow in the casket.

And there she lay. A woman I knew, had seen standing by the downstairs door waiting for her ride almost every day, had spoken to almost every day for years. Fragments of conversations slipped and slid into my mind, ricocheted: *Hello. How are you. Fine, thanks. Have you had a good day. Take care. Have a nice weekend. My, that's an awful cold you've got there. I hope you'll feel better soon. Good morning. Good night. Goodbye. Goodbye.* I had never known her name. *I had never known her name.* A nice woman, a small woman, friendly in an acerbic way, sort of a beaky, birdlike face, sort of a wiry quality about her, sort of a nasal rasp to her voice: someone I liked. I never knew her name.

Very funny things were going on in my mind. Not shock; no, not that; remember, we have a lot of deaths. More like, *well, for heaven's sake, so that's Wilma Bremer.* But I never knew her name. *(Lord, can I ever be forgiven? There are so many, Lord. Answer from Lord: There is only one of each.)*

But I give myself full marks here, after all, I am a pro—and like all of us, proud of it—all this didn't take a second. I didn't miss a stroke. "Yes, Gerald," I said, "she looks very nice. They've done very well for her."

"Does she look like, you know, *herself?"* asked Gerald. "Does she look, um, *natural?"*

"Oh, yes," I said. "She looks like herself." She didn't. Dead is dead. But I got inspired suddenly. Go for broke. We rehab types are gamblers too, good at long shots. "Why, Gerald," I said, "she looks better *than herself. She looks much better than natural . . ."*

Gerald was utterly delighted.

"Oh that's *so nice,"* he said. For a second he forgot the appropriate low tone and his voice squeaked high. *"Oh isn't this nice, Joan?"*

"Really nice, Gerald," I said. *"Really* nice."

He rubbed his hands together briskly in his great satisfaction. "I suppose we should go," he said, with regret in his voice. "I suppose we are holding up the line." I had a second of panic, a feeling that he would have liked to stay there more or less permanently, I could see the two of us stuck there through eternity, holding Wilma's hand. *(Would that do it, Lord?—is that what you want from me?)*

"It's all right, Gerald," I said. "Nobody minds. Wilma doesn't mind. God doesn't mind." (I frequently take it upon myself to speak for God in my capacity as therapist—yes, I am that too, rehab demands great versatility—well, hell, I feel that anybody alive has the right to speak for God. Or as God.) I glared around at the whole damn church, screw you all, back at Vange too, she was probably aware of the whole thing, she usually is (I am God, but she is Buddha, God is really a lot less effective in many situations), and she was probably laughing at me.

But we did go back to the pew, knelt. In an excess of terrific enjoyment, Gerald reached out and groped for my hand, found it and pressed it, squeezed it. "I don't believe I asked you this, Joan," he said: "Did you know her?"

"I knew her," I said. *I just never knew her name. I never asked. Did she know mine? Perhaps; even probably; because I am important, I am a supervisor in rehab. It is now too late. Sometimes it is too late. I can never, ever, in all of time, say the thing that would have been right: Hello Wilma.*

Hello Gerald. Hello Vange. Hello Lou, hello Bob, hello Jenny. Hello Sharon, hello Bruce, all you dying sons of bitches, all you dead alive, all you beautiful. Hello. Hello.

IX

As it mentions in some religion or another, *the ineffable name of God that no one can utter* (The Rumpelstiltskin of religion?):

perhaps it is Wilma? or Gerald? Danny? Fred? Barbara? even Greg? or—God help us all—Jerry? Some dumbhead at Social Security? How can you know? Be safe—remember all the names. Try. Take note of all the people. Look at the faces, if you can see. Remember. Do your best. It counts. It does count. Maybe nothing else counts.

X

Vange remembers all the names. Even all the voices. Do you recall that I told you somewhere in the middle of this story that I was going to say more about this? I told you not to forget? If you forgot, you will think this is anticlimax, but I tell you I know what I am doing, trust me.

Don't permit yourself to get sidetracked by all the foregoing religious hysteria, grief, shock, etc. That is not the story. This is the story:

Once I was in a restaurant in New Ulm, Minnesota, with Vange. It was called the Kaiserhoff. A waiter came up, spoke to us, asked what we would like to order. He had a European accent, which I could not place. It wasn't quite like Peter's, it wasn't Lithuanian, but it was a little like that.

Well, suddenly I saw Vange do her thing. It is funny to see, but at the same time it is rather alarming. Her face becomes very flat and smooth and her eyes narrow behind her glasses. A perfectly deadpan expression comes and then a little smile, lips together: totally smug. In fact she really does look like the Buddha at these times: she is fat enough for it too.

Vange said: *Why I think I remember you. Weren't you the young man who helped me find some noodles in a National Tea store one night about fourteen years ago in Devil's Lake, North Dakota? I asked you where the noodles were and I told you I was a little blind and couldn't find them myself and you were very nice and took me right over to the shelf and found the right kind of noodles for me? And your name is*—pause—oh god, the suspense was incredible, could she really pull this off?—*George!*

Well, you *know* that waiter was absolutely knocked out. He said he did remember, she was right, he remembered her, it was his first night on the job, he was just over from Estonia, and he remembered the blind lady. Of course, of course.

Well, it was like Old Home Week. Nothing was too good for us from then on. They stuffed us like we were a goose for royalty. I will never as long as I live forget the deep-fried sauerkraut balls. Some things I do remember.

You think this cannot be true, but I am telling you it *is* true, this did happen. Well, I told you that Vange was a genius—of some kind.

She is also very hard to take. And she probably set blindness back a hundred years in New Ulm, they probably think she could do that because she is blind. I promise you that these things do not happen because she is blind—they happen because she is Vange.

I tell her that what she has is a gift, a talent, and she can't take any credit for it. She says it is not a gift, it is a matter of paying attention. I do not want to believe her; but I think I do believe her. A little.

Goddammit, I'm like Social Security: I do the best I can. I do try harder though since Wilma's funeral.

(Vange put the clincher on Wilma's funeral. She said, when she read this story, I'll bet you never noticed that Wilma had a hare lip, did you? And what do you supposed I answered? Well. You know me a little by this time, don't you? I am like you. No, I never noticed.)

THE NIGHT CLASS

What exactly is art? I have been wondering in some depth about this question lately. Who am I to ask such a question at all, you want to know: a *social worker?* They say a cat can look at a king, dearie. And I am, no matter what Richard Nixon said about us social workers—and after all, what's *his* credibility?—a card-carrying member of the human race; so far as I know, Homo sapiens is the only species on earth that produces anything that it dignifies by its own consensus with the name of art.

As a member of the human race, then, I am going to focus on this question, which has been bothering me like you can't believe. Ever since my back went out, as a matter of fact, while I was hammering and chiseling away at four a.m. on a Saturday trying to get a plaster cast of a fullsize portrait sculpture out of its plaster mold.

I took a class in portrait sculpture this past spring in a local high school's night program. There were six of us and the teacher. For eight weeks, one evening a week, we each modeled a clay head on a wooden armature, and then we made a mold over the wet clay, and then we cast the head in plaster inside the mold. Sounds simple enough, right? It was a bitch.

Our model was a young woman named Joanne. She had her

hair cut in a smooth, boyish style—her features were rather like a beautiful boy's features, too.

"Build from the inside out," the teacher told us. "So that you've got a feeling for the inside. Build the brain and the blood vessels and the blood and then the skull; understand that the brain and the blood and the shape of the skull are under there *before you do anything else . . .*"

Well, I doubt that at first any one of us had a clue as to what she meant. I mean, there we were, a couple of housewives, an elegantly dressed receptionist for a fancy apartment complex, a young engineering consultant, an elementary school teacher, and me, a social worker. I did not understand her; but I *sort of almost* understood, can you follow that? It was like some far out place in my mind caught just a glimmer, a faint dim light, of her meaning; like there was in me a capacity for understanding that had been poked delicately from a distance, and that stirred and tried to wake.

There were mutterings. "What does she *mean,* I don't understand . . ." wailed Frances, the receptionist.

Melissa, a small, sturdy housewife, sweet and quiet, looked frightened. "What does she mean?" she whispered.

"Just do it," the young teacher, Liz, said. "Just believe me. Just make your hands do what I tell them to, and after a while you'll get it. *Believe me.* You *will get it.*"

Well, we tried. We did what she said; she was an extraordinarily compelling young woman, this Liz. In the right circumstances, I believe she could have been another Hitler. We did what she said. We covered the upstanding twelve-inch pole of the armature with clay. Then we built it out. The neck is too thin? *Build it some more.* Build. Build. She never said model, she never said sculpture, she said build. And she said *work* a lot, too.

And work it was. At the end of the first night we each had an enormous head-shaped object on our wooden armatures which we all (five middle-aged out-of-shape female would-be artists and one young male: the engineer) carted about half a mile up and down stairs and along halls to a storage space. It was awful. I thought for sure I would drop the goddamn thing, or succumb to high blood pressure. I am after all forty-eight years old, and have a rather sedentary occupation. A dialogue went on in my head:

Margaret: Remember, Mother, you're in the heart-attack age.

Me: Kid, stuff it.

Marg: But Mom, you're *always* saying that your back is going to go out. *This is gonna do it . . .*

Me: Yes, but what can I do?—I can't *chicken,* for god's sake, everybody *else* is doing it . . .

I didn't drop it. *I didn't drop it.*

This went on for eight weeks. On the third and fourth nights we got to the point where she let us begin to "build" the features on our sculptures. Everyone of course saw the model differently, and everyone had a different sort of portrait. I, for example, "saw" Joanne as a young Amazon warrior, and I made her boyish hair into a helmet. I have been reading women's movement literature for the first time in my life recently—I seem to come to many things late. I think the reading informed the way I saw our model.

When I had one side of her face finished—the forehead, one eye, one brow, the delicate nose, the voluptuous mouth, the firm, strong jawline, the stubborn chin—when I had one side, the right side, more or less finished, an odd thought crossed my mind: I will leave the left side unfinished. It will be more interesting that way.

But then I thought: but I'll never know what the left side would have looked like if I stop now. I'll never know whether I *could* have done it.

So I finished it. And I want to tell you, that left jaw was *hard.*

I built. I cut away. With a kitchen knife. Built again. Cut away. Built. The eye was pretty easy, but the jaw was murder. It took me most of one evening to get that jawline; but I did get it. One second it was a sculpture in process; and the next second it was finished. I put my knife down.

"Liz," I called. "I think it's done."

She came over. Looked at it. "Are you satisfied?" she said. "Yes," I said. "I'm satisfied."

"Wonderful," she said. "Now you can make the mold."

Make the mold. I stared at her. "My god," I said. "I forgot there was more." She laughed, this little black-haired, round-faced, round-eyed Attila. "You've just begun," she said. "Listen, art is hard work."

I've just begun. Art is hard work. Build from the inside. Build. Work. Do it.

Didn't this little dictator understand that I had worked eight murderous hours already that day? I mean, anybody who thinks that social work is easy should try it for a week or so.

She looked at me, and her look was absolutely merciless, but kind of cheerful. Come on, it is going to be fun, that look said. So I made the mold. It *was* fun. It was also work. And it was dirty work; I had plaster all over me, I must have looked like a statue myself. I ruined my good Rubbermaid dishpan mixing the plaster. My hands hurt and burned with stiffening plaster.

"Art is also dirty," said Attila. "Just let the plaster dry on your hands until it comes off easily." Just let the ants eat your flesh until they get to the bone. Simple. Nothing to it.

"There is *no clean art,*" said Attila, the artist, firmly. Exhorting, encouraging, bucking up, challenging, daring, and bullying her six more or less willing slaves—let me tell you, this kid was something. She could make artists out of cadavers. And she damn near had to. But we kept coming back for more. She had promised us something. She had promised us that if we did it we would understand. She said we would "get it" if we just did it. She had said a magic thing: *Believe in me.*

One of us—Frances, the neat and tidy apartment-complex receptionist—held out for a while. She glared at the little teacher with eyes that were getting bloodshot, what with the plaster dust and all: *"There are some arts that are cleaner than this one,"* she said. She was dead game though, Frances, after she had registered her protest: she kept coming back. A miracle—they all came back, week after week; there are almost always dropouts, in any night class; no one dropped out of this one.

The last night of the class, we were not quite finished. But we had to take our projects home anyway. Mine was a plaster cast of my lovely Amazon inside a plaster mold two inches thick. The whole thing was at least fifteen inches high and a good two feet in circumference. And heavy, my god: it must have weighed fifty or sixty pounds. Maybe more. I put my arms around it to pick it up and carry it to the car. And there was simply no way in hell I could lift that thing.

I mean, folks, I am a small person. Short. Thinnish; well, I try. Sort of weak. I have a large and strong self who lives inside my unsatisfactory body; people are always expressing surprise when they meet me in person after, say, phone conversations or letters. "Wow, you're so *little,*" they say. "I thought you'd be this, like, *huge person . . .*"

Let me tell you, whoever you are: *I'm* not altogether pleased with this envelope either.

Anyway, I finally asked the grubby, plaster-sloshed young engineering consultant (Martin, his name was) if he would help me, and between us we got that incredible lump, looking like the Frankenstein monster before they took the bandages off, into the trunk of my car.

"Goodbye, everybody," I called—they were all out in the

parking lot like me, stowing their creations in their cars. Considering what we had all shared for eight weeks, "goodbye" didn't seem good enough. *Let's get together? See you in hell? I'll never forget you?* Maybe—but not goodbye.

Why, I *loved* those people; I had to embrace them all; then they embraced each other; then we all got into a circle and were really together. We must have been a sight: seven plaster-covered sculptors—counting the teacher—in the moonlight, in a circle arm in arm. I hated to leave. But you always have to leave, or be left, one way or another; a little practice along these lines is never wasted.

II

So I drove home. No way, of course, could I get the sculpture out of my car. I was too tired; I would worry about that tomorrow. I had a couple of cans of beer, relaxed into utter hand-trembling exhaustion, and fell asleep about ten p.m.

It must have been one a.m. when I woke up like a shot. Tomorrow! But my beautiful girl was in that plaster mold *now! I had to get her out.* I went out to the car in my pink and green flowered robe and slippers, and opened the trunk. I tried to lift the sculpture out. I could move it a little, but I couldn't begin to lift it. I tried and tried. No way. Then I remembered about people being strong enough when they had to be. I thought about it: and decided: this definitely was such an occasion. I mean, I really needed to get that damn thing into the house. "God," I said, as firmly as I knew how, "please let me lift this son-of-a-bitch and carry it into the house."

And what do you know, I did it. I got the thing up, into my arms, down the driveway, up the steps to the front door, I balanced it on my knees while I somehow got the front door open. I brought the thing into my living room, to the tiled entryway.

And that was the end. I couldn't go any farther, I put it down (lowered it by agonizing inches) onto the floor.

I should have said basement. Godammit, I should have said "into the basement." In my prayer. I never think far enough ahead. But one miracle a night is all anybody is entitled to, the way I saw it; no way was I going to try that again. In the living room my girl stayed, while I got out my hammer and chisel and screwdriver.

So there I was, at two a.m., give or take half an hour, in my middle-class living room on the tiled entry floor, by the open staircase, across from the white fireplace wall with the andirons and the glass doors and the whole bit, and the just-refinished oak floors, hammering and chiseling away like crazy. And crazy is what it was: I couldn't *not* do it. I was compelled and obsessed. The first blow that went deep enough to break away a big piece of the mold and uncover a quarter-inch of the sculpture underneath was an unbelievable triumph. If I remember correctly, I yelled "Hallelujah!" and ran around the room jumping up and down. Really, I guess I was nuts.

And then I got back down to it. Place chisel, tap with hammer, swear—and uncover another microscopic bit. Marvelous. I uncovered the whole back of the head by four-thirty a.m. Then I cradled my beautiful Amazon face up in a bed of towels— there was plaster all over the room by this time: ground into my new woven-grass-rug, trucked into the kitchen: I had to have a drink of water every once in a while, didn't I? Jesus Christ, even *Rodin* had to have a goddamn drink of water occasionally.

I knew I was making a horrendous mess. And I didn't care; I know myself, I was pretty sure that I would care in the morning, when I came out of this, but right now I didn't care. Right now, all that mattered was that my darling was under that plaster, I had to get my darling out of her plaster prison. I mean, I was *into* this.

The hardest part was ahead of me—to carefully chip out that delicate face, the tender line of brow, the smooth forehead, the overhand of helmet-hair, the intractable sensuous mouth, the fine, strong, stubborn line of jaw and chin. Oh, I had a picture of it all in my mind, and I had to see it in the flesh. Well: in the plaster.

But suddenly I hit a terrible block: I was afraid. I was afraid that I would break some part of the beautiful face I remembered. I did the right side of the face first, I worked around the easiest parts, a piece of the neck, the very beginning of the jaw by the hairline, the overhang of the helmet of hair, the forehead, some of the line of cheek and temple; I uncovered the right brow. It was as beautiful as I remembered it, I could have absolutely kissed it. Maybe I did kiss it, how would I know?—I mean, I was—do you get this?—*beside myself.* I was absolutely nuts; I was absolutely into this thing. Beside yourself is when your self is here, on the living room floor, working (delicately now, with the littlest screwdriver, the lightest touch of the hammer) at the very outer edge of the right eye; and you are somewhere else and God only knows what you are doing. I maybe kissed that eyebrow.

And from the multiple tracks into the kitchen, I knew the next day that I drank a lot of water.

But the outer edge of the right eye was so fragile; how could I do it? With only a hammer and a chisel and a screwdriver? Brain surgery with a kitchen knife?—I couldn't do it. But something interesting happened. A voice inside of me said: dear God just let me get this one upper eyelid out unhurt. Tap. Tap. Tap. Oh. Scrape. Careful. And there was the eyelid, maybe fifteen minutes later. A great truth was dawning—I didn't have to do the whole face, I only had to do the eyelid. Then I only had to do the eyeball. God, just let me get the eyeball. That's all. Only the eyeball, God.

For you to realize how extraordinary this was for me, you have to know that in all the years of my adult life I had before this only prayed in any formal sense twice: once for my son to live and once for my father to die.

It didn't work either time, but that is beside the point. The point is that I saved prayer for really special occasions. Compared to life and death, what was this? But here I was on my hands and knees on the tiled entry floor of my living room, in a really uncomfortable position, automatically praying over one piece of this sculpture after another. I wasn't thinking of praying, I was just doing it. Ok, Lord, now *just* the inner corner of the eye. Ok, Kid, we've done it, now *just* the right side of the nose, ok? Be careful—oh. Beautiful. Now the curve of the upper lip coming down from the nose. Now that delicate indentation from the upper lip to the middle of the nose. Now—Lord—listen, this is going to be a real biggie—now the mouth. *Just let me have the mouth, Lord.* I got the mouth out. Was I happy? No. Happy is ordinary. *I wasn't anything ordinary.* Understand this.

Another part of my mind (besides the part that was praying, the part that was directing the hand holding the chisel, the part that was making the hammer fall just right, the part that was exulting every time another bit of the face emerged unhurt, and the part that was registering the fact that my back was hurting a lot and I had plaster dust up my nose and in my mouth) another part was off on its own kick. It was thinking about a short story I had read thirty years ago, called "Head by Scopus." In this story a beautiful young man had lupus; one side, the right side, of his face was perfect; the other side was made a ghastly ruin by the disease. A split-off part of my mind was absolutely focused upon this story.

Well, she was right, Liz-Attila-artist, she promised me true. I had got it all right. But what I had wasn't (or maybe was, this was however beside the point) a beautiful work of art; what I had was obsession. I could shake hands with Rodin now, or

Michelangelo; I could say to them: We know what we are. We are laborers, and possessed by our labor. We are mad. As fucking hatters. Maybe hatters have it too. In their way. Maybe the way doesn't matter. Maybe the only thing that matters is *getting it.*

It was broad daylight by now, about ten o'clock on that Saturday morning, and I was just too tired to do another stroke. I took off my glasses and rubbed my eyes with plastery hands. Surely I couldn't lift that hammer one more time. And I had the whole right side of the face uncovered, freed. And it seemed beautiful to me.

But I just couldn't stop. One more stroke. I put the chisel against the left side of the mold, at random, going for nothing, and hit it with the hammer. Just a light tap, no harder than any that had gone before. And my God, the whole mold shuddered, was loose. I put the hammer and chisel down. Wiggled the piece of the mold that was left, gently. Yes—yes—it was definitely loose all over. Was I going to luck out? Was I going to be freed thus easily from the rest of the labor that so possessed me and was at the point of killing me? or at least throwing my back out? A reward for diligence? God, it was about time.

Sure enough, I lifted the remainder of the mold away in one piece—from the neck, the whole left side. And stared at what had happened. Part of the left side of the face had broken off, was still stuck in the mold: half of the left eyebrow, the eye, the cheek, and the jaw up to the nose and mouth. But it broke in such a way as I could never have dreamed, never intended. The accidental break was perfect, the lines of the break were perfectly beautiful. Head by Scopus. Who was the artist? What was the art?

III

Several years ago an art exhibit came to Walker Art Center in Minneapolis. The title of the exhibit was "Naives and Visionaries." Maybe you saw it. It was, I believe, displayed in many cities around the country.

Perhaps it was the most extraordinary exhibit ever put together, anytime, anywhere. I can't imagine what would tie it, unless it would be a collection of Ilse Koch's lampshades, something along those lines. But unlike Frau Koch's artwork, this art was innocent: absolutely and totally. Or—was it? In a way it seemed also evil; perhaps total innocence contains or implies or allows a kind of evil. It was certainly mad. And it scared me a lot.

I went with my friend Maeve. She made me go; I was busy that summer, I didn't have time. But she said it was a collection like no other—of tremendous works, incredible undertakings, by people who were not artists, and who worked in no understandable medium, for no understandable purpose. She really forced me to go, Maeve did.

We walked in. The first exhibit was a room full of—dreams. I mean, I recognized them immediately as representations of dreams, I am after all a therapist, some of the time, anyway, and I hear a lot about dreams. But these were crazy dreams, such as few of us ever remember in the morning. It was like when you suddenly see a person and you know you have never seen that person before, and yet you know that person. You *know* that you know; but with a different kind of knowing.

I *knew* those dreams. The impact was astonishing. Maeve and I both felt it—we kept touching each other, it was like we wanted to keep in contact with what was familiar, what we knew was sane and real and ok. But we were dazzled.

"Maeve," I remember saying at one point early in our mesmerized viewing. "Surely these people were touched by God. . . ."

There was an old weather-beaten board, maybe four feet in length, stuck upright. And slipped over the top of the board, shaped to bend over and point with one finger, was an old rubber glove. Pointing the way to the rest of the dreams—to the terrible, terrible, wonderful dreams.

There was a garden—of sticks, with decapitated dolls' heads impaled on them, growing in bouquets, like unholy flowers.

There were intricate mosaics made of thousands and thousands of discarded pencils stuck together into designs that covered whole walls.

There were houses, rooms, built of bottles: one room of glass bottles called "Cleopatra's Bedroom." There were photographs of creations too large to move, ever: a "Garden of Eden" in concrete: huge concrete animals and plants. Pictures of enormous towers, great walls—made of junk, the discards of this civilization.

Well, Maeve and I were absolutely knocked sideways. We kept talking to each other at first—"Marvelous! This is marvelous! These people were real artists . . ."

But what they did, didn't fit. It was screwy. After a while we didn't talk anymore. After a while we were speechless: what was there to say? *For sure it was art: for sure: and for sure it was crazy.* After a while we were really scared, I think, at least I knew I was, I really wanted to run, the goddamn thing was coming too close; there was something too alien here that was at the same time absolutely familiar, absolutely human.

We stuck it out, though; actually, I think we were afraid not to. We were afraid of rejecting these awful dream-things; if we rejected them, there was something wonderful that we would also lose.

I think the worst exhibit, and the most wondrous, marvelous, was an altar done in aluminum foil. It took up a whole wall of one room, and stuck out into half the room. It was made up of very ordinary objects, chairs, tables, vases, mirrors, frames, lamps, God knows what all, probably can openers, and every surface was covered with aluminum foil. It was simply amazing; I mean, there was just no question about it, the thing *was art.* The man who did it *was an artist.* Ordinary objects from ordinary life were transformed into something wonderful—what else could it be, but art?

But the sign underneath told us that the man who did it didn't stop with an altar. He covered, I mean, *everything* with aluminum foil. He went into his garden and covered the living flowers and the blades of grass, and the separate leaves of the trees, with the shining silvery foil. Well, but was it art *then?* But what else could it be? There were pictures of the garden; it was beautiful.

I knew a woman once, her name was Rosamund, who was very, very beautiful—everyone who knew her agreed that she was. She had a sister who, feature by feature, looked exactly like her. But the sister was ugly—everyone agreed. In Rosamund, it worked—in the sister it didn't. What was the difference? A slight change of a line here? Or there? A fraction of an inch difference in the placing of the eyes? You simply couldn't say what the difference was. But the sister was ugly. But who said so? What is the standard? Do we just *know,* from all eternity, what is beautiful and what is not? Or do we decide? Or are we ignorant? Or blind? Are small bits of stone or glass truly better than pencils? Is gold leaf better than aluminum foil?

Maybe there is a pair of human eyes in this world somewhere that will one day look at Rosamund's sister and say—"My God, how beautiful you are!" And maybe after that we will all see differently. Perhaps this person with eyes that see beauty where ours see none will be a very powerful person, an artist, or an emperor, and he will teach us to see what he sees, or decree that we shall see it. And will we then look at Rosamund and say: *Yech?*

When Maeve and I left the museum, and breathed ordinary air again—it felt like that, like the air inside was miasma, poison, wonderful, but poison—we didn't talk much about the exhibit. We talked about other things, ordinary things. We stopped and had a cup of coffee. *A cup of coffee:* my god.

But I was telling someone about that exhibit recently (I tell a lot of people about it—the thing haunts me) and I told this person that the thought in my mind when I got out was: *God, just don't look at me.* The person I told said: Perhaps He already has. Perhaps you're done for.

Art is obsession; recognition is when you luck out in a cultural consensus. But art is itself: alone, lonely, packed in a trunk, never seen by any except you: art is what you do that satisfies you. Liz-Attila-artist said true. "Are you satisfied?" she asked. "Yes," I said. "I am satisfied."

Maybe I'll quit my damn social work job and go to art school. Maybe Richard Nixon—I am crossing my liberal fingers behind my back, folks—maybe R.N. had a point.

THE SUN, THE RAIN

Rosealice came to us off the street.

Who is "us?" We are an agency for the rehabilitation and employment of blind people. There are other kinds of handicapped people working here in addition to blind folks: deaf people, people who do not speak or who have speech impediments, Hmong refugees we were asked to take in because they do not speak our language yet; people with brain tumors, people who are what is called retarded, people with cancer, epilepsy, cerebral palsy, whatever: people broken, ill, crazy, or otherwise deviated in any one of a hundred ways from the golden, sound-limbed, competitive standard that we say in this country is normal.

All of these people are supposed to come to us by referral, from the State Office for the Blind, or the Department of Vocational Rehabilitation, or some other such agency. The reason they are supposed to be referred, instead of just coming in by themselves, is that we need a lot of preparation to be sure we are doing the right and best thing in each case rather than just dishing out spontaneous good will: we need eye reports, medical reports, psychologicals, authorization, work histories, Individual Written Rehabilitation Plans, etc., etc. The human services professional, in spite of the high place we accord him or her theoretically, cannot—if you judge by our systems—be trusted any farther than you can spit.

Since we need all this paper to keep us on the right track, there must of course be someone to send it to us; therefore we need referring agencies.

Well, but nothing is easy these days; I guess you know that. I mean, you live in "these days" too. You are normal, or you say you are, but even so you need a lot of paperwork to make it through. Things are not simple anymore. Maybe there are just too many of us now for simplicity.

Me and Vange figure that we own this agency. We are social workers. If you know any social workers, you will know that they all tend to think that they secretly run things, that the people who ostensibly have the power couldn't get along without them. Vange has been here for nearly twenty-five years, me for only ten, but I am Vange's boss. This is hard for people to figure: Vange is so much smarter than I am, why isn't she the boss? Because that's the way it is, that's why. I have the right paperwork.

People are people, though, they simply will not or cannot be orderly, follow the rules all the time, and so sometimes handicapped people come into our sheltered workshop without any paperwork. Social Service is constantly bitching about this. As a matter of fact, I am the head of Social Service: What the hell is going on here? I say to Marlin Jenkins, the workshop director. Why did you let this person start working without coming through Social Service? Well, Marlin will say, but we didn't know: he didn't tell us that he was legally blind. Or epileptic. Or crazy. Whatever.

Sometimes we advertise for sighted people in the newspapers, or put a sign in our front window: some percentage of our jobs do require sight. We hire these people without any credentials at all: off the street. That is what Off the Street means: that people just decide to ask us for work on their own initiative. And Rosealice came in one day off the street. Our window sign said Clerical Help Wanted, and she walked in and said she typed eighty-five words a minute, and that's how we got her. If Jack the Ripper could type eighty-five wpm, we'd have hired him too.

Upstairs (in the Rehabilitation Center, which is supported financially in part by the sheltered shop) we heard about her before we saw her.

They've got a very strange new typist downstairs in the Production Office, Vange said one day. She types eighty-five words a minute error-free. Her name is Rosealice.

Rosealice? I said. One word? Like you said it? Rozallis?

Right, said Vange. Ro-Zallis.

What an odd name, I said. I never heard that name before.

Well, she's an odd person, said Vange. Maybe she has an odd name because she's an odd person.

Anybody who can type eighty-five words a minute error-free in this building is odd all right, I said.

I made up a reason to go down and see Rosealice. We are like a small town here, or a family; all of us are intensely interested in anything unusual that is going on anywhere in the building. So I took some stuff to be typed and went downstairs and asked Jan—the production coordinator—if I could use her new typist: Annette is snowed under upstairs, I told her.

Jan said it was ok to use Rosealice.

Take it in and tell her I said it was all right, she said. It might take you a little while to explain to her just how you want it, though. She's kind of different, Jan said.

So I carried my stuff into the room next to Jan's office, where the typewriter was banging away so fast it was almost a steady noise instead of your usual plock-plock-plock. Hi, I said: you must be Rosalice, I'm Joan Shepherd, I work upstairs in the Rehab Center, how are you, welcome, I'm real glad you're here: well, you know, all the things I would say to anybody new. I mean, you can't scare me with "different"; listen, we are practically immune to "different" here; we have, you might say, built up a tolerance.

The typewriter stopped. Brown eyes in a large, pale, square face looked up dazed from the copy. H-hello: she said. Her mouth bent into a stiff parody of a smile. Hello, I said again. Do you like it here so far? I said. I l-love it here. she said: everyone is so kind here. I am very hap-happy here. She spoke very fast, the words came out like bullets, and her stammer was like bullets too. Her eyes homed in on mine and locked. I felt like I'd been shot dead center. Honestly, Jesus: what an impact she had on me. Well, and you don't expect that, do you? I mean, people just don't look at other people like that.

And there was a problem all right. That became clear right away. It was like she couldn't hear me; really, literally, not hear; though she wasn't deaf or anything like that. And she was very scared. I had to tell her the same things over and over, and even then she didn't get it. Finally—I don't claim this was inspiration, actually it was more like despair—I took a pen and sort of drew on the copy the form I wanted the final product to have. And that she understood.

Oh! she said, and her face cleared a little, the awful concentration lessened for a second. *I see!* And she took a pen and the copy, and I stayed with her while she read the thing aloud all the way through—hesitating and stuttering in fear, but stubborn, my god, intense—and she wrote over my neat little penciled corrections with the heavy black pen: she wrote large, bold, black. And then she typed it up absolutely perfectly, with a perfectly even touch. It was beautiful—and listen. she did it faster than the speed of light practically.

She's visual, I told everybody: that's the thing, she is absolutely and totally visual. You just have to show her, draw it for her, and then she's ok.

It wasn't that simple, of course, but that was the heart of it.

She didn't get on well with Jan. Rumors kept drifting up, mostly via Vange.

Jan says she doesn't think Rosealice will make it in the Production Office, Vange said one day.

You're kidding, I said: we get somebody at last who can type eighty-five words a minute, and Jan thinks she won't make it? You've got to be kidding.

Well, that's it, said Vange. She can only type, she can't do anything else. Jan needs somebody who can do all sorts of things, filing and all the rest of it, not just typing.

My god, I said, how silly can you get? *Jan* can do the other things. This agency *needs* a typist who can do eighty-five words a minute; I mean, *desperately.*

Well, yes, Vange said. But another thing is, Jan can't stand her. There's something too strange about her. Jan is thinking that if she doesn't work out as a typist, maybe they could use her on one of the assembly jobs in the workshop.

My god, I said: when we need a typist so badly, they'll take one like that and put her on *assembly?*

Well, said Vange. There's nothing wrong with assembly. And she likes it here. If Jan can't use her . . .

That's not the goddamn point! I said.

You know, I was furious. I simply can't stand waste. I am very efficient, very compulsive.

Well, in the end I saved her for typing. She's upstairs with us now, at the desk by the dictaphone. She's up to ninety-five wpm, and climbing. And she has learned braille by sight. She does most of the brailling now for our blind staff members and board members. She learned braille faster than anyone ever did before in our experience: well, I knew she would, she is a natural, her eye-hand coordination is fantastic.

And she loves brailling. She learned it just in time to meet the demands of our eight new blind board members who insist upon having everything, I mean *everything,* in braille; well, but you know, it's right that they should have it, isn't it? It's just that before Rosealice, we simply couldn't keep up with it.

I really think that in a manner of speaking God sent her to us. She is so useful to us. She answers our needs perfectly. And we answer hers. Perfectly.

Rosealice is a large woman, heavy, strong, built like a longshoreman, like a stevedore. On the job she had just before she came to us—we only know a little about this, Rosealice doesn't tell us much about herself—she did some sort of clerical work on a loading dock. They made her lift heavy things, she says. She didn't like it. Her face grows dark and tense when we ask her about that job.

All the secretaries are nice to Rosealice. I have made this happen. I have explained her to them, explained that she is different, and how she is different. I have, you could say, sold her to them: well, though, this is my job, selling people to other people. And to themselves. Listen—I will say—underneath what I conceded is a grisly exterior, there is a poet, a flower, a really lovely person . . .

Rosealice did things at first that nearly blew the whole project. Annette came into my office one day to talk to me about it. She sat at my desk with her hands folded primly in her lap, looking the picture of the perfect secretary.

Um, she said. I really like Rosealice.

Out with it, I said: how can you like her? She's awful.

Well, not *awful,* said Annette. Not exactly.

Her hands began to twist together.

Oh, come on, Annette, I said: of course she's awful. I think you and Jennifer are doing a wonderful job to put up with her at all.

Well, there *is* a problem, said Annette: two problems, in fact. Two main problems . . .

Ok, I said. What are the problems?

Well, said Annette. She keeps asking questions. She asks things that she knows already. She asks about everything, every other minute. Sometimes she even asks the same question over and over. Me and Jennifer can't get our work done, she's driving us crazy asking questions.

She's afraid, I said. I'll fix it. What else?

She coughs, said Annette. She's got a terrible cold and she won't stay home and she coughs and spits into this handkerchief, and it is all wrinkled and dirty and it's making us feel sick . . .

Oh, I said. Yes. That's harder.

Can you make her stop? said Annette.

Oh, yes, certainly, I said. I can do that.

So I talked to Rosealice. Vange and I talked to her together, actually. We told her that we liked her: if that was a lie, it was meant well. We said that she was doing a great job. We told her that we really wanted her to be able to stay with us. We told her that there were certain ways in which she would have to change if she was to stay.

Oh, I w-want to stay, said Rosealice: I know you girls will tell me what I have to do so that I c-can s-stay . . .

So we told her, and we laid down some rules. You must not speak to Annette and Jennifer *at all.* For a while. We will be your supervisors; you must come to us. You must not ask questions when you know the answers; *you do know the answers, you are intelligent.* You must go across the hall to the bathroom when you have to cough. This is what the world wants of you. Conform or forget it.

I am intelligent, she said. Smiling grimly, concentrating. And nodding. Getting her head around it.

I must not speak to Annette and Jennifer.

I must come to you. Or Vange.

I must go into the bathroom to cough.

Well, it sounds bad. I know it. But it was necessary. Dammit. And right. And we meant well—God sees the heart. And she thanked us; listen, she practically blessed us. You girls are my guardian angels: she said.

Anyway, it worked; she stopped asking so many questions and she coughed in the bathroom.

Were her feelings hurt? Annette asked me.

No, I said. Not at all.

What did she say?

Well, she thanked us, I said; she was grateful. Really, it's ok, Annette.

I feel so bad about it, said Annette.

Darling Annette, not twenty years old; with your heart-shaped face and serious smile.

You don't need to, I said.

I don't understand, said Annette; I'd be so hurt.

There was also the question of the "highwaters." For a long time, Rosealice wore her polyester pants hemmed up with about eight-inch hems, so that the pants were six or seven inches shorter than was fashionable.

The secretaries appealed to me: Joan, they said, can't you convince her to stop wearing those highwaters?

For heaven's sake, I said. What do you want from me? I made her stop coughing. I made her stop asking so many questions . . . I felt really irritated about this.

Besides, I said: what have the highwaters got to do with her *job?*

Nothing, I guess, Annette said. But they make her look different. They make her, I mean, she doesn't *fit in . . .*

Fitting in, apparently, is important. And the secretaries are right—it isn't the quirky mind, or the agonized face, or the heavy worker's body—it's the highwaters.

Vange says: The thing is, the secretaries are right, the highwaters, I don't know how it works, they make her look retarded.

What is going on here? Vange loves the retarded people, why does she worry that the highwaters make Rosealice look retarded?

Well, maybe it is this: that Rosealice is too close to what *we* are. The retarded people are obviously totally different from us, we do not have to acknowledge relationship to them. Could that be it? Isn't that obvious?

Her face: I didn't really tell you much about her face. And now that I've thought of it, what can I say? Well, it is a large face. Square. Worn: she is only two years older than I am, she is fifty-one, I know this because I have reviewed the paperwork on her; but her face is terribly marked by whatever her life has been. It is a strong face, pale, with no makeup. The large features are not intrinsically ugly, but there is an effect of ugliness. This face is twisted and squeezed inward at all times in what appears to be an agony of tension and uncertainty; it never relaxes, it varies only between tension and more tension. This is true even when she types or brailles: both things she loves doing.

When she smiles, it is worse. Her smile is a crucifixion: she seems to be in terrible pain when she smiles. The skin of her face is very tight and shiny. The smile breaks it into planes and lines, and whatever light there is slides from plane to plane on her face

like little lightning. Why: the smile itself is like a dreadful light.
She says she is happy. She says so all the time. She keeps saying it. To anyone who asks. Or who will listen.

And—this is a strange thing—I believe that she *is* happy; it is
not a lie. She is not deluded.

She *is* happy; she really is happy, I said to Patsy Aaron, our
tutor in the rehabilitation center.

Yes, said Patsy, I think you're right. I think she is happy. But
there's something else wrong: with me: her happiness makes me
want to cry.

A few weeks after Rosealice came, Vange and I gave a
Tupperware party. You know about Tupperware, I assume; is
there anyone reading who doesn't know about Tupperware?
Well, but years ago I didn't know about Watergate until it was
almost over—maybe there is someone out there who finds it as
difficult to keep track of this civilization as I do. "Civilization" is
the focal word here: not knowing about Tupperware is an anti-
cultural position.

Well: so then: Tupperware. Tupperware is a ritual of this culture. Sort of like Social Security. Tupperware is important: a
focus for a ceremonial gathering together of people who do not
especially want to be together so that they may buy—at a rather
high price—an excellent plastic product that they basically do
not need and do not want. People are told when they are invited
that they don't have to buy this product; however, it is a strong
and renegade individual who can hold onto an intention not to
buy. Dessert is served, and coffee. There is a saleswoman present
who demonstrates the plastic product and takes orders. I have
never heard of a male Tupperware salesperson; and I don't know
that there has ever been a Tupperware party for men. Funda-
mentally, it is a female rite.

You get something at a Tupperware party that is not in the

description of what happens. I think you get a guarantee of commonality: we're all in this together, and we are all alike: there are no outsiders here.

Well, Vange and I are students, undeclared, of civilization and its peculiarities; so when we observed that the workshop people were at one point feeling left out of things, we hit upon the idea of a Tupperware party to bring back a feeling of community. We invited all the blind women in the workshop; plus those from other departments: otherwise who would the workshop people feel community *with?* We invited our own department of course—Social Service—and everyone who had any remote connection with Social Service, the intake people from the rehab center, for example; and the tutor, Patsy, who doesn't exactly belong anyplace in particular and who might very well feel left out too; and all the secretaries from everywhere in the building because hardly anybody ever considers them. That's how Rosealice happened to come: she got lumped in with the secretaries.

When it came right down to it, we invited fifty-two people: a simply monstrous Tupperware party. Well, but only thirty-nine actually came: thank God, says Vange.

Patsy Aaron was sitting next to Rosealice in a big circle—actually a double circle, there were so many of us—around Vange's living room at the Tupperware party. I overheard a conversation between Patsy and Rosealice: clear, between the words of other conversations, you know how this will happen sometimes in a crowd, one thread will suddenly emerge as separate from the whole, and all the rest will seem muted.

Rosealice: I think this is wonderful don't you just w-wonderful?
Patsy: The party, you mean?
Rosealice: Yes I think it's so w-wonderful that we are here that Vange asked us to come here Vange is wonderful. Rosealice's voice is tense and urgent and happy: she speaks in a stuttering

loud monotone.

Patsy: Yes, Vange is a nice person.

Patsy's voice is light and intelligent, as always.

Rosealice: Oh no Vange is *wonderful,* everything is *wonderful,* everyone is *wonderful,* just *wonderful.*

Patsy: (laughing) Well, I don't know about *everything.* I don't know about *everyone.* . . .

Rosealice: Oh—yes: everything. I think we all have so many reasons to be happy. For example, we have the s-sun, the sun shines, and I think that's so wonderful, and we have the rain . . .

I decided to rescue, that is after all part of my business, rescuing: Listen, Patsy, I yelled across three other people: don't sweat it. The sun will probably fall out of the sky tomorrow . . .

Patsy: laughing: in relief: Oh, *right!* We don't have to be happy after all, terrific, tomorrow the sun will fall . . .

Across three people I saw uncertainty in Rosealice's face. Oh, no, she said: the sun will still be there tomorrow . . .

I was ashamed. Yes. I was. I do have a capacity for shame.

But listen, what else could I have done? Could I have let Patsy sit alone confronting this dreadful heresy, that we should be happy *because we have the sun?*

The next day Patsy came to see me in my office.

How did Rosealice get like that? she said. I mean, you're a therapist, you ought to know.

Oh, sure, I said: I ought to know. She's crazy, I said: that should be obvious.

Yes, but, the awful part of it is, the thing is, she's *right.* Said Patsy. She's right and we're wrong.

Oh, well, yes, I said: that is certainly true. Absolutely. (Ha-ha. I am in my sarcastic mode.)

Patsy: I mean, we *should* be happy, we *do* have reasons to be happy.

But we're not, I said.

No we're not, said Patsy.

And that's normal, I said. What we are is ok. What she is is not ok.

But that's terrible, said Patsy. That's so sad.

Me: Oh, yes. That's terrible. That's sad. Oh, yes.

How did she get like that? Patsy's question. Well, I don't know; Patsy thinks I ought to know but I don't.

I make something up for the secretaries. You know, I say to Annette, really terrible things have to happen to people to make them like Rosealice is, we don't know what happened to Rosealice, and we probably never will know, but the thing is, if we are kind to her she will be happy here: and she's worth it, she's so useful to us, nobody works harder, or better. And I guess we can stand it to have one happy person here.

That fact is: Annette says: the truth is. She gropes for the words. Finally: I couldn't get along without her now, she says. I don't know what I would do without her now.

We get clues. Not very many. A few: startling.

One morning I was humming something when I went into the secretarial area.

Are you happy today? said Rosealice to me: You must be happy today.

Happy? I say: Certainly not. *(You take that back immediately:* is the thought in my mind.) What makes you think so?

You're hum-humming, says Rosealice. Her voice is cracking with anxiety.

I think that one over. I believe you're right, I say. I feel surprised. An answer occurs to me: I believe it must be because it's Tuesday, I say: I have always liked Tuesdays.

She jumps on this enthusiastically, like a dog onto a wonderful bone: Oh! she says. Oh! I have always liked Tuesdays too!

Is that so? I say. I am paging through a book of records. The paperwork here is driving me absolutely up the wall: it seems to be increasing geometrically lately.

Oh! Yes! she says. In fact I wrote a song about Tuesday when I was a little girl, it went like this, *On Tuesday . . . a bear ate . . . my . . . brother . . .*

She sings it: a simple delicate complicated melody.

I look at her. I don't very often look right at her, it might burn my eyes I think. Jesus, I say: that's a great song, Rosealice, I could have written that song. When I was a little girl.

I can remember being a little girl; but the concept is strange to me in relation to Rosealice. She could not have been a little girl, it is out of the question.

When Rosealice had worked for us for thirty days, she was—as all of us are upon completion of thirty days of work—inducted into full status at the agency via the ceremony called Getting Onto the Insurance Plan.

I gave her the plastic Blue Cross card that signified her initiation.

Here you are, Rosealice, I said. Keep this in your billfold and then if you get taken to a hospital or something you've got it.

What is it, she said. Taking it from me and turning it over and over in her fingers.

It's a card that says you are covered by the agency's insurance plan, I said. When you work here for thirty days you get on the insurance plan.

Insurance plan, she said.

Yes, I said, you know, when you get sick now you don't have to pay for it if you go to a doctor: You're covered. Eighty percent.

I'm covered, she said. She sounded scared.

I took a deep breath. Covered, I said, means that you are in our health insurance plan, you're a member of it. Like the rest of us.

Are you a member, she said.

Yes, I said.

Oh well then I guess it's all right if you are a member too, she said. Is Vange a member.

Vange too, I said.

Oh then it's all right, she said.

Yes, it's all right, I said.

I told Vange about it afterward. I don't think she knew what insurance is, I said: listen, Vange, is that possible, that she didn't know that? My goodness, said Vange. My word.

I ride the same bus with Vange coming to work every morning. The 7:41 a.m. 4J. This bus picks me up practically right in front of my house and drops me off across the street from the agency. I get to work about one minute before 8 a.m., the official starting time, which is about as perfect as you can get. I could drive, but taking the bus is so easy. Obviously, as a manager, I could come in late, but I don't; I am much too neurotic for that. Well, I am scared, you see; this college master's degree and this manager's job came on top of too many insecurities for me ever (apparently) to feel that the degree *and* the job were anything but accidents.

The 7:41 is almost, but not quite, as convenient for Vange: she walks a block and a half from her home on Aldrich Avenue to ride it.

Sometimes Rosealice gets onto our bus at Lake Street. I believe she takes another bus from St. Paul: I have that impression. I have never actually asked her, though.

Vange and I sit in a front seat that adjoins a long seat to make an L shape along the side of the bus right up to the front door. Whenever Rosealice sees us she plunks down right by us on the long seat. Always. If the nearest place is taken, she stands by us, grabbing a hand hold.

W-well, hello there! she says. Shouts, actually. Rosealice always talks in a very loud voice.

Hello, Rosealice, we say distantly, hoping everyone will notice the dismissal in our voices.

Rosealice chatters on and on. She says the same things again and again.

H-hello.

H-how are you girls?

Isn't it a, isn't it a, lovely day?

Have you, have you, have you—*staccato, well I told you before, like bullets*—read any good books lately? (Yes, honestly.)

Isn't it a lovely day?

Etc. Etc.

Vange and I (by tacit agreement, it is not spoken or arranged) decide to sit farther back on the bus. Rosealice never sees us back there. I suspect her eyesight is not very good.

We both feel guilty as hell.

Why are we doing this, Vange? I say. When we feel so guilty about it.

I know, says Vange.

But why, I say.

Well, we are avoiding a scene on the bus, says Vange. We are being thoughtful of our fellow riders.

Sure, I say.

She's too different, says Vange: We can't stand her.

But we like her, I say.

Oh yes, says Vange. Liking is one thing. Conversation on the bus is another. Knowing her is another.

Not *like*, I said. *Love.* I *love* her. Don't I?

Yes, I think so, says Vange.

Why, I say.

She means something important to you, says Vange.

When I see her typing upstairs in the morning, I feel happy, I say. It's like walking into the sunlight to hear the sound of her typewriter. Honest to god.

Maybe she's my happiness, I say.

Maybe she's my sun.

Maybe, says Vange.

I told you before, Vange laughs at me.

She's certainly your responsibility, says Vange: you saved her.

When we go by the secretarial area now, we can hear the sound of Rosealice's typewriter banging away. It does not sound like the other typewriters. Well, the other typists, as it happens, do not want to be typists. They want to be: social workers, counselors, managers, recreation directors. They are discontent with what they are: they want to be something more, something other. They are in a way full of envy: they envy us, the social workers, etc.

Rosealice likes being a typist; she says she does. Oh I love typing, she says; when we ask her. What about brailling? I ask her. Well, brailling too: she says. Which do you like best, brailling or typing? I ask her. Well, both: she says: I like them both. I have upset her a little, though: when I asked her to choose. Her forehead creases in an anxious frown. She finds her solution, and the cloud clears: I like about half of each, she says. Every day.

The sound of Rosealice's typewriter is a happy, tearing-along, going lickety-split, rhythm, music sound.

She's very lucky, says Vange.

How so? I say.

She really likes to type, says Vange. She really loves it. She has found her niche. It's a pleasure to walk by and hear that sound.

I tell Rosealice that. Vange says it gives her pleasure to hear the sound of your typewriter: I say to Rosealice.

Oh, I love to type: says Rosealice. It makes me happy to type: she says.

Yes, I say, that's what I'm saying. It is very clear when you type
that you love doing it. It makes us all feel happy too, that you
are happy.

I just love to type, says Rosealice firmly. Her smile, that agonized cracking of the tense mask, hurts me. I go away. She goes
back to her typing. The sound is happy again. Tap-tap-tap.
Hap-hap-hap. Tappy-tappy-tappy. Blessed are the: how does it
go: For they shall see God? Or something. Wow. This track
could take you anywhere. You could trip out on this: I could.
Nevertheless, I do not want to be a typist. I do not want to be
what I am, though, either. If you give me my heart's dearest
desire, whatever that might be, I think probably I will not want
it after all.

Rosealice dresses kind of funny. I told you about the highwaters.
Well, there are other things. Sitting and typing and brailling and
being happy, she is getting fatter. Her winter coat—which seems
to be made of good wool, it has a good label, Peck and Peck, we
can see the label when she hangs the coat in the secretaries' clos-
et—her coat does not close anymore across her big body.

She wears a strange hat. It is a child's hat, I think.

One afternoon she rides the same bus with me and Vange
going home. It is a cold day. I am sitting at the front of the bus
and Vange is next to me, on the inside of the double seat. Large
Rosealice is looming over us. Rosealice wants to stay by us, she
holds onto a pole by us. The bus gets crowded, people have to
push past Rosealice to get on at all. She will not move back. She
carries a purse and a black metal lunch box such as a manual
laborer might carry. She has an awful time juggling the purse
and the lunch box and the pole, the hands that type so capably
are clumsy in this operation. She is wearing the coat that will
not close, and her funny hat.

It's very cold today, she says. Smiles eagerly. Breathes audibly.

We are communicating, the smile says: isn't it wonderful?

Mm, I say: Cold, yes. My tone is discouraging, I feel. I do not want to communicate.

I am not cold, though, she says: I have my hat on.

Mm, I say.

My warm, furry hat, she says.

Mm-hm, I say.

She *will* tell me, though. I cannot stop this thing she wants to tell me.

It makes me look like a kitten, she says.

I look at her. The hat is a hood or bonnet that ties under her chin. There is a wreath of fur that goes around her face. Her large white face smiles and simpers inside the wreath of yellow-tan fur.

Maybe a lion, I say. *Maybe a werewolf, I think.* I feel grim. I am always grim at the end of a day. I do not like my job. I want to be a hardware sales clerk or something. Maybe a mail sorter at the post office. But this hat idea somehow interests me, I am attracted by it.

No, a kitten, she says. A nice little kitten. She nestles her face coyly into the fur ring. She bridles and preens. Smiles. Nestles. I am a kit-kitten, she says.

So. This big, strong, white-faced typist-braillist is a kitten. I shrink down a little inside my coat. I am embarrassed.

She babbles on: I am a kitten, I am . . .

All the other people on the bus are watching, listening.

Listen, suddenly I want to tell you, the fact is, I personally am a giraffe. No, listen, I really mean it: *I am a giraffe.* In my imagination, I can hook into giraffeness. I have always known this. Did she buy the hat because she knew she was a kitten? She did. Oh, yes, I know this.

Thank you for telling me, Rosealice, I say.

To hell with the other people.

But I do not tell Rosealice that I am a giraffe.

In a way, though, you know, I can after all see her as a little girl. When I try. I can see her under a tree: in a garden. The sun is shining. There are flowers all around. There is a stocky, plump, black-haired, brown-eyed, happy and strange little girl. She is about six years old, I think. She is singing: *On . . . Tuesday . . . a bear ate . . .* etc. She is touching the flowers and speaking to the sun, she is an intimate acquaintance of the sun. There is always a boy present, the boy is older. The boy is cruel, he hates the little girl. He teases her: always. Nyah, nyah, nyah, nyah-nyah-nyah, he taunts her. You are fat. You are ugly. He pulls flowers from their stems. He tears them apart. He throws them at her. Fix them, he says. She tries; but who can fix a flower? She is crying. You are stupid, he says. Then he gets tired of his game. He runs away.

Actually I am making this up. All I can really see is a little black-haired girl sitting in a garden. Under a tree. And the sun is always shining. Or else it is raining.

I suppose I should confess: there are things I know in myself that are involved in the way I feel about Rosealice. I understand about the typing, for example. It has always seemed to me that if I could only find the one thing I liked, really *liked,* to do, that then I would be happy. And I am clear on this: that the thing does not have to be big or important. What I envision when I think about this is building little houses out of toothpicks: I do not mean that I actually want to do this, I only mean that it would be all right to want to do this. There would be no moral lack involved in wanting to build little houses out of toothpicks instead of wanting, for example, to be a doctor or a politician— just to pick out at random a couple of important ambitions. Other people could choose to be doctors; in my imagining, being a doctor would be every bit as good as building little houses out of toothpicks. But—and this is the point—it would be no better. There would be no value attached. Only happiness, if you could call that a value: happiness would be the value. Are you happy? would be the question.

I notice that I have inadvertently hit toothpick-house-building rather hard. I wouldn't want you to get the idea that I really want to do that. It is just a metaphor. A symbol. Whatever. Actually, I think that particular thing wouldn't suit me; I think I would get tired of that pretty quickly.

Do you know the idea of God's Fool? This idea runs throughout the literature and myth of western civilization: maybe through every other civilization's literature and myth too, I wouldn't know about that. But the God's Fool is sort of a happy simpleton: he goes his own way. He (or she, obviously it can be a woman too, like for example St. Therese, whom they called The Little Flower, I am named for her, Joan Therese, my given name is), anyway, the God's Fool smiles a lot. He never judges the rest of us: I expect he thinks we are rather wonderful. But he himself is humble; he is not in any way conceited about his own gifts, whatever they may be. He is usually intent, this simpleton, upon some task which is pretty much beside the point.

I guess the juggler of Notre Dame was a God's Fool; juggling balls in front of a statue for the glory of God, my word. My goodness. Francis of Assisi: he must have been one of them. Candide. The Fool in the Tarot. Blake. Albert Einstein? Johnny Appleseed? Why not? (Do you remember the song we used to sing when we were children about Johnny Appleseed? Something like this: *The Lord is good to me . . . and so I thank the Lord . . . For giving me . . . the things I need . . . the sun, the rain . . . and the appleseed . . .*)

Listen, this is an important question: could typing be something a God's Fool would do?

Once I had a notion at the back of my mind that I ought to end up as a God's Fool, was meant to be one. Do you think you can choose such things? The problem with the idea of being a God's Fool, though, is basically a socioeconomic one: I mean, who ever heard of a God's Fool owning a house and a car and a color TV, or working as a manager? I guess it's hopeless, this secret notion of what I was meant to be? Well, why do I ask you—of course it's hopeless. I am as bad as Rosealice with my questions.

What do you think, Vange? I asked one day. Do you think a person can choose to be a God's Fool?

I don't see why not, said Vange. What do you want to know for? Why are we discussing this?

Do you think I could be one?

No way, said Vange.

Why not?

Well, she said: for one thing, you lack humility. For another thing, you have too much money.

I guess that's true, I said. Both of those things are true.

I know Vange thinks I am getting a little peculiar. I catch her looking at me funny every once in a while. Well, Vange loves me, you know. She wouldn't want me to go off the deep end or anything, or do anything that was actually going to hurt me.

She has nothing to worry about. Obviously. Since I lack humility and have money. And I am not about to take up the one and dump the other. Being a God's Fool or any other kind of fool is not an option, goddammit. I'm unhappy with the way things are, all right, but I'm not that unhappy. I'm no more unhappy than anybody else. Do you think? What do you think?

Annette meets me and Vange at the door as we come into the building one morning. She is very upset, she can hardly get her message out fast enough.

They're going to take Rosealice away from us, Joan! she says.
Vange! You have to do something!

What in the world, I say. Vange says.

It's true, says Annette. Why, Annette is almost crying. She says: I got here early and Greg came up and told me.

Greg is the director of the rehab center: maybe I told you that before.

That's crazy, I said. Why would they do that?

The new blind board members don't want her, Annette said. Because she's not blind. They think she should be blind. That's what Greg said.

Well, I was simply knocked over. Vange! I said. Do you know anything about this?

Vange always knows things ahead of time.

I did hear a rumor, she said.

Why didn't you tell me? I said. Yelled. God. I was so mad.

Rumors aren't always true, Vange said. Mostly things like this don't actually happen.

Is this one going to happen? I said.

I think so, says Vange.

No it's not, I say. I'll stop it somehow.

You have to tell her, says Annette. She is really crying now into her little white lace hankie. I can't tell her, she sobs.

She is not going, I say. I won't have to tell her. Nobody will have to tell her.

I put my arms around Annette. Don't cry, darling, I say. I'll fix it. Everything will be ok. You'll see.

But everything wasn't ok. I couldn't fix it. The blind board members won, and Rosealice had to be told that she couldn't braille and type for us anymore. I told her. Like Vange said, she was my responsibility.

Do I have to leave here then? she asked.

You can go into assembly if you want to, I said. In the work-shop. With your eye-hand coordination you'd probably make as much money there as here. Well. More. Probably.

Oh, thank you, said Rosealice: I don't have to leave you all. I can stay here.

Honestly. She didn't seem to care at all about the brailling and typing. It was—apparently—us that she loved.

Rosealice doesn't have to leave; but I am leaving. I can't stay here anymore. I am going to go out and build toothpick houses. Well: I'm going to art school, is what I am really going to do. I suppose I can get some kind of part-time job. Or I can live on my savings. For a while.

I thought Rosealice would be upset when I told her I was leaving, and she was, but the news didn't kill her or anything. Will you come back to see us sometimes? she asked.

Probably, I said. (Though I am not the sort to come back, that is not my style.) But: Certainly, I said. I promise. Of course. Of course I will.

Well, then, that's all right, she said: Will Vange leave too?

No, Rosealice, Vange will stay, I said: Vange and I are not Siamese twins, we are not joined at the head or anything. I do lots of things that Vange doesn't do. And vice versa. Vange does lots of things I don't do.

I think of you two together, said Rosealice.

Well, we are together, I said. Sometimes. Sometimes we are separate.

Oh, well then, that's all right, Rosealice said. If Vange doesn't go. She smiled: that terrifying smile.

She's on assembly now. She went on before my scheduled time to leave. I was able to set that up anyway. Lose the war and win the battle. I should tell you that I've given the folks here six weeks notice; well, you know, I've liked it here, even though I did complain a lot, and I thought I owed them that: six weeks notice. I thought, you know, that it would be hard to replace me. I thought I was terribly good at what I did.

Actually, there's talk of not replacing me at all.

I've seen Rosealice in the workshop every day since she went there. The line leader says she learned astonishingly fast: nobody faster, ever. She's up to $8.43 an hour already, which is more than she'd ever make upstairs as a typist.

Do you think you can be happy here, Rosealice? I say.

Oh, yes, she says. She stops twisting the little piece of wire on the object that she is assembling. She smiles, and her face breaks again into that mass of shiny planes and the light from the over-head fluorescent bounces and slides off the planes and lines of her face. I'm ter-terribly happy, she says. The people here are all so n-nice. Mr. Jenkins is so nice. And V-Vange comes.

You know, I'm jealous. Just a little. She was mine before and now she isn't. You now? I mean, I'm glad for her, but I'm also just a tiny, teeny bit jealous. But I forgive myself. I was only human after all, I say to myself. There, there, dear: I say. To myself.

I'm going to art school. I guess I told you that. When I leave. After art school, who knows? You never know about human beings. They can surprise you.

I figure I'll have to cut back some while I'm in school. I probably won't be able to afford to drive the car, for example; when you really sit down and figure it out, cars turn out to be terribly expensive. Maybe I'll just simplify things: and I already know a lot about getting around on buses. So maybe I'll get rid of the car altogether one of these days. One of these fine days when the sun is shining. Or when it's raining.

THE HARDWARE STORE

Several days, maybe a week, after her name was first mentioned to me I suddenly had what I thought might be a memory of Alicia.

The memory had a quality of vision: there came, tilted in out of nowhere, an image, a picture. A woman's head and upper body, still and clear as in a photograph—pale flesh and black hair and blue denim overall, tarnished brass buttons and eyes flashing a dark and hostile awareness at me—a clear and focused picture in my mind. I stopped what I was doing, struck: why, I said to myself, that might be Alicia. I think I remember Alicia.

I think I remember Alicia, I said to Charlotte at work the next day.

Well, sure you do, said Charlotte. You would. I'm sure you were living here before she left.

Living here. You heard that? We work at Gelle's Hardware Store on the corner of 28th and Delaware in Minneapolis—me and Charlotte and Mac the fixer and the rest—and we all live within a block of the store. As a matter of fact, one of the reasons I was hired is because I live on the block.

Oh! said Sandra, one of the owners, the day I was hired: Oh, I knew that if I just waited long enough, the exactly right person would walk in the door!

Charlotte looked dubious.

As it turned out, they were both right. I *am* exactly the right person for some things.

Not for others.

Sandra thoroughly dislikes me now. And is very uneasy with me. As I am with her. And Charlotte and I get along wonderfully: we laugh a lot and discuss Sandra when Sandra is not there. Not all of our discussion is complimentary. Charlotte is a little more cautious than I am. Well, she has to stay here and work for a while longer; I don't. I am flattered that she trusts me as much as she does.

I am going to art school in March. The hardware store is only a stop-gap for me: a temporary resting place, an oasis. I am resting here between the events that belong to my real life.

I wait for the day—it will never come—when Sandra says to me: what do you think of me?

I think you're a cold rigid bitch Sandra: I say in this temporarily favorite and permanently hopeless fantasy. Hopeless: no one ever really asks you what you think of them. No one that you want to call a rigid bitch, anyway.

I believe I came to the hardware store as a consequence of the direct intervention of God's hand in my life. I am that kind of person: I believe in things. Like Direct Intervention. D.I.

I was a social worker—a kind of an odd one, but nevertheless certified. I worked with blind people, most of whom had other handicaps in addition to blindness: diabetes, MS and CP, age, deafness, lupus, mental retardation, you name it. Brain tumors. Cancer. It began to seem to me one day that I would go crazy if I stayed any longer to stare into the wide-open unblinking eye of human pain. Maybe I was a little crazy, had already become so, that is. So I quit my job. A few days later I was walking past the hardware store and thinking—this is true, I am not making this up—"I have always wanted to work in a hardware store. . . ." and there was a sign in the h.w. store window: Help wanted, 11 a.m. to 4 p.m., M-F. So I walked in and asked about the job and Sandra hired me on the spot. It was clear to me that she thought I was a D.I. too.

II

The hardware store was a neighborhood institution when I moved onto the block, and had been, people told me, for about seventy years. The store is located right next to Mellison's grocery, which is also an institution.

The hardware store was owned at that time by an elderly man named Benjamin Gelle, assisted by Charlotte, Alicia, et al. I don't really remember much about what Gelle's was like then; except I do know that it is a lot tidier and a lot less interesting now.

The present owners, Sandra and Ron Acheson, kept the Gelle name when they took over. They told me when I first came to work—when they were still trying in their way to communicate with me, had not yet given the whole thing up as a bad job— told me how they had changed the place after they bought it. It was really terrible, said Ron: the only person who could find anything was Charlotte. We waited until Charlotte went on her vacation (he said) and then we put all the stock into boxes and ripped out all the shelves and put in new shelving and reorganized everything.

The new shelving runs in two straight lines of tiers rising almost to the ceiling. There are three aisles the length of the store, one on each side and one in the middle, separating the tiers of merchandise. It is fairly clear where things are: every item is ticketed and numbered with an A-1 Hardware price sticker, and behind every group of items—say a hookful of carded measuring spoons—is a little pasteboard tag, maybe one by three inches, with a matching A-1 sticker on it. That way, when you run out of measuring spoons, you can look at the sticker and get the name of the item and the price and the order number and you can order more spoons and put them right onto the same hook when they are delivered and unpacked.

This is a good system. It should work and for the most part it does. But it depends a lot on human beings 1) doing what they are supposed to, and 2) being totally knowledgeable about the general areas and categories where things ought to be hung, stuck, placed, piled, etc. This is almost never the case: there is always somebody like me who can't tell a measuring spoon from a shovel and sticks up a new hook for the measuring spoons over in the shovel area. And there is always someone like Charlotte— well, let's face it, there is Charlotte—who thinks the whole system is largely bunk. Well: anathema.

And when the system breaks down, you end up with an empty hook in housewares with a spoon-ticket on it; and Ron doing the order on Friday when the ordering is done and seeing that empty hook and that spoon ticket; and ordering spoons; and then finally you get a lot of new spoons on Tuesday when the order comes in. To be—once again—placed with the shovels by some dummy: me. Or some subversive: Charlotte.

One of the reasons I was so dumb for so long at the hardware store was that nobody was very good at teaching. Take the cash register. Sandra taught me to use it the first day I came.

Have you ever operated a cash register before? she said.

No, I said.

Ok, she said: you punch this—clunk—and—quick quick mumble mumble *zip*.

That's all there is to it, Sandra said. It's really very simple, you won't have any trouble with it. She said. And left. Briskly and competently bounced out the door. On her way home? (Sandra doesn't live right on the block like the rest of us do—she lives a couple of blocks away.)

Quick quick mumble mumble *zip*. Clunk.

Charlotte, I said, when Sandra was safely out the door: I am afraid to tell you this, but I didn't understand anything Sandra said, and I don't know how to operate this cash register.

I didn't think you were getting it, Charlotte said. Sandra goes too fast. She shows you too much at once.

Well. Charlotte said. This is a new cash register. I hate the damn thing. I don't do it like Sandra says to. I don't understand that way. This is what I do.

So she showed me enough to get by.

Doing things Charlotte's way got me in trouble many times with Sandra. It didn't get Charlotte in trouble of course, because Sandra needs Charlotte.

In the end I more or less had to rely on the idea that if I was indeed here by Direct Intervention, then God would help me with the cash register. And if I wasn't (here by D.I., I mean), well then, the hell with it. And everything worked out about as well as it had to.

There was also learning the names of things. I had to fill out charge slips—Gelle's made a lot of its money by its charge system, hundreds of people had charge accounts there. And in order to fill out the charge slips, I had to know what things were called.

Hey, Char, what's this? I would call out.

That's a connection, Charlotte would say.

Or an adaptor, or whatever.

Hey, what's this now, Char?

Um—a connection, she said.

Finally she said: Anytime you don't know what something is,

you can call it a connection. You're always fairly safe calling it a connection. She said.

Fairly safe—that seemed to be sort of optimum in the h.w.s.

III

One Monday a couple of weeks after I started working at Gelle's, Sandra said to me: Alicia came in Saturday looking for her stamps.

Stamps? I said.

And: Who is Alicia? I said.

It's my fault, said Sandra. I should have told you.

It's remarkable how you can be accused by someone who says: It's my fault. Have you noticed this? You wouldn't think that would be an accusation; but it is.

What did I do wrong? I said, panic-stricken. Now you might ask yourself—why should anyone be so scared of this Sandra person? You are sure, you think—I imagine you think—that you would not be. The reason is simple: I am out of my familiar element here. I am a fish out of water. On the esoteric beach of the hardware store, I flop about not knowing the rules: therefore it is possible that I break the rules without being aware of them, every time I turn around.

What did I do wrong, I said.

Oh, nothing, said Sandra; it's my fault, I should have told you.

But she accused me. I wanted to cringe. Well: I did cringe. Obviously.

Alicia comes in most Saturdays, said Sandra. She comes in to get the stamps from our envelopes. I believe she saves the stamps for her nephew.

Stamps, I said.

Mm-hm, said Sandra. Every time you do the mail, you should save the envelopes. And put them all in a paper bag.

Doing the mail was one of my designated tasks—in fact it was the only one I had that was mine alone, that no one else had too.

Sandra bent over behind the counter where the paper bags were kept. She picked out the right size bag. She took a piece of the morning mail—which had not been done yet—took the enclosed check and statement out, processed them quickly, and stuck the envelope into the paper bag.

Like that, she said.

Oh, I said. Like that. Ok.

Sandra went on, explained more fully. I always save *all* the envelopes, she said. Even the ones that are machine processed. Sometimes Alicia saves postmarks too.

Save all the envelopes, I thought. Ok. Yes. Why not.

Who is Alicia, I said.

Alicia used to work here, said Sandra. She worked here for years.

Thirty-seven, said Charlotte.

Thirty-seven years, said Sandra. She recently had a series of little strokes and she can't make herself understood at all now when she talks, she comes in here and writes out on a table what she wants to say. It's kind of pathetic. Said Sandra. In her brisk practical no-nonsense voice.

She spent most of her life in this hardware store, said Charlotte. Thirty-seven years.

The bag was stuffed full by the end of the week. I opened the envelopes as carefully as I could so as not to tear either the postmark or the stamp, and I saved every one of them in the paper bag.

Do you have to save them all? asked Charlotte, about Thursday. Can't you just save the interesting ones?

Sandra said to save them all, I said. I'm just following orders.

Charlotte was quiet for a while, cleaning the light-bulb shelves, dusting off the bulbs. Charlotte works very hard, not so much because there is a lot of work to do—there is a lot of work, but this is not the point—as because it is in her to work hard.

Then: Sandra wouldn't know, she said. How would Sandra know? If you didn't save them all?

I'm taking no chances, I said: I'm saving them all.

Oh, said Charlotte. Well. That's probably wise.

See? Even Charlotte: brave and true and wise and good: isn't sure what lurks.

IV

Charlotte. I think you should meet Charlotte more formally now. If there is a meaning to this story, Charlotte must be part of it.

Charlotte represents—it seems to me—the continuity in the hardware store. She has worked here for twenty years, except for a six-week break five years ago when Ben Gelle angered her to the point where she actually quit. Then when Sandra and her husband bought the store from Ben, just a few weeks later, they went to Charlotte and hired her back.

Would you consider coming back to work? they said to her. (She tells me this.)

If I don't have to work Saturdays, she said. I will.

Ok you don't have to work Saturdays, they said. Except in emergencies.

So she went back to work, has been back here now for five years.

What made Charlotte quit was this: she tried out the question about working Saturdays on Ben Gelle, and Ben said Certainly You Have To Work Saturdays You Are Not Worth The Money I Pay You Anyway. So Charlotte quit. A look of shock comes onto her face when she remembers this.

Char says that Ben had a party for her before she left, and at the party he told everybody that she was the best employee he ever had.

That was Ben's way, she says. All of it was just his way.

But even understanding that, she got mad and quit.

I think Charlotte loves the hardware store. I'm not completely certain about this, but I think so.

One day Charlotte accepted a screened baby crib to be repaired—the hardware store, in addition to selling many thousands of useful items, also does repairs of various kinds.

The crib was hand-made, screened with copper screen. The edges of the screen were fixed into about a dozen hinged panels by means of strips of wood fitted into quarter-inch-deep squared indentations around the edges of the panels. Between each strip of wood and the inside of an indentation was caught an edge of screen. The crib was lovely and eccentric, and very difficult to repair, particularly with the steel screen we had, which is nowhere near as strong as an old-fashioned copper screen.

Charlotte seemed uneasy about this object, which over several days of inquiry we found out was for use in the southern part of the United States, to keep black widow spiders away from a sleeping child.

Mac can fix this, said Charlotte. Mac can fix anything. Mac is really good.

But somehow the time went by and Mac, who is the best of the store's fixers, didn't fix the crib. Personally I think he was afraid to try, afraid that he might ruin it. Charlotte became increasingly anxious about the crib. One night she dreamed how it could be fixed. In the end, she and I fixed it together. It took many hours. There was no way we could charge what it cost us to do it. We had a wonderful time. It was so hard. The screen kept breaking. We were I think a little hysterical by the time it was finished.

I don't know another hardware store in town that would have

done that, said Charlotte. Fixed that.

Think of it another way, Charlotte, I said, teasing: Is there another one that would have wanted to?

She stopped, struck. That's true, she said. This is probably the only hardware store left in town that cares to do things like this.

That's something, she said, softly, and to herself: to work in the only hardware store left like that . . .

Well, the hardware store is Charlotte's. This is very clear. It doesn't matter who owns it, or who gets to keep the money. Such things are completely beside the point.

They don't understand what they've got in you, Char, I said one day. When you leave they'll find out that you really were the store. It'll be nothing without you.

I don't think that's true, she said. People used to say (Char said) that Alicia could never be replaced. But she was. By me. Said Char.

V

Sam was in on Saturday to get the stamps, said Sandra on the Monday following the first week I saved stamps in the brown paper bag.

Sam, I said. Who is Sam?

Alicia, Sandra said. Alicia Samson. Everybody calls her Sam.

Oh, I said: ok. *Sam.*

She hates to be called Sam, said Sandra. She wants to be called Alicia.

Why do they call her Sam then? I said.

Because she looks like a man, said Sandra. She is very tall and built like a longshoreman. Years ago she did all the really heavy work around here, people used to say they couldn't tell whether she was a man or a woman. Said Sandra. In her brisk, informed voice.

Didn't you ever see her? she said. A great big woman, dressed in an old bib overall? I believe she was here until about a year before we bought the store.

Maybe I did, I said. I must have, I said.

Sandra was just about to leave (she spent very little time at the store, really) when she turned back and said: about the stamps. You should throw out the ones that are machine stamped. Sam won't want those.

That's what I always do, she said.

Other people began to ask me about Alicia when they found out that I worked at Gelle's Hardware Store. There was for example a woman named Carol whom I met at a party:

Gelle's Hardware Store! she shouted. God! I have always *loved* Gelle's Hardware Store!

It is pretty marvelous, I said.

God, said Carol. They've cleaned it up though, haven't they? Since Gelle sold.

Oh, I said. Yes. Some. It's still pretty much of a mess, though, I said: Charlotte tries hard to—um—preserve some of the old ways. I laughed.

Charlotte, said Carol. She's the young, pretty one?

Well. She's fifty-eight, I said. Pretty, yes.

Does the great big woman who knew where everything was still work there?

That must be Alicia, I said. No, Alicia doesn't work there anymore. They talk about her a lot, though. I save all of our stamps for her, she comes in on Saturdays to get them, I said. I don't work Saturdays, I never see her.

God, and I never *will* see her: I don't work Saturdays, I thought.

She was something, said Carol. She was as strong as a man and she knew everything in the store, she could find everything.

She knew more than Gelle. Said Carol.

The store won't be the same if she's not there, she said.

No I suppose it isn't the same, I said. It's still good though.

I drive by sometimes, said Carol. It looks neater. The windows look neater.

Well it *is* neater, I said: some. But listen, it's still not *fatally* neat or anything like that. I mean, Charlotte says it is known in the trade as The Pits of A-1 Hardware. So it can't be *too* neat, I said.

It's a shame, though, to change it at all, said Carol. It was a great store. It was perfect. God. They had *everything*. They could do *everything*.

It's Sandra and her husband who want to clean it up, I said. It isn't Charlotte. Listen, they waited until Charlotte went on vacation to put the new shelves in. The reorganized all the stuff while she was gone.

Presented her with a fait accompli when she returned, huh? said Carol. God—she said—that's sick.

Sick. I never thought of it like that. Hm.

Charlotte said that actually they did not finish the shelf reorganization while she was gone; they just started it, got it to the point of no return, so to speak.

It took months, said Charlotte: to get all the stuff out of boxes. We were unpacking the stuff for months, she said.

Oh, the store didn't yield so easily then, I thought. Pleased.

VI

By and large, I found the people in the hardware store relatively insensitive to each other compared with the human services types I had been dealing with on my other job. The aluminum window fixer, for example, got sick one day, had to go to the hospital. We heard this via the neighborhood grapevine. No one from the store called to find out how he was, or what was wrong.

How's Loren? I would say every day when I came in.

We don't know, we haven't heard, someone would say.

Didn't anyone call to find out? I said. Really, I was shocked.

Well. No. We didn't call.

One day I looked up Loren's number and called his home. I talked to his wife.

I'm Joan Shepherd, I said, I work at Gelle's. We are concerned about Loren . . .

His wife seemed pleased that I had called. She said she'd say hello for us to Loren in the hospital. She said he'd be glad.

Loren has diabetes, I told Charlotte when I worked with her next: I called and talked to his wife, I said.

You *called?* said Charlotte. She looked puzzled.

What made you call? she said. Were there windows to do or what?

No I just called, I said: I *like* Loren. I was *interested.* I was *concerned.* So I called.

Hm, said Charlotte.

I told his wife to tell him hello from all of us, I said. I told her to tell him we were concerned.

Sandra sent a plant to Loren in the hospital today, Charlotte told me the next day. Fifteen dollars, she said. A poinsettia. Can you *believe* fifteen dollars for a *poinsettia?*

Wow, fifteen dollars, I said.

That's giving from the heart all right, I thought. Meanly.

VII

Information, data, about Alicia came in bit by bit.

You already know that she was a big woman. Who looked like a man and did a man's work. Was called, by some, Sam.

And wanted to be called Alicia. Not Sam.

But there is some more for you to know. She taught Sunday School at a Congregational church for thirty years, for example. (Charlotte tells me this.) People whom she taught as children remember her still, write to her still and send her stamps from all over the world. She has told Charlotte this.

Thirty years.

Something odd comes in here. Ron and Sandra were both teachers before they bought the hardware store. Charlotte tells me one day, for no reason at all, connected I mean to nothing that I can see, that after Ron left teaching, some of his junior high school students came by the store to see him: to say hello.

They still come, she says: once in a while. Some of them.

He must have been a good teacher, she says. They wouldn't do that unless he was a good teacher.

They must have liked him a lot, she says.

I suppose it is possible that Sandra is ok too. Unless Charlotte is wrong? Charlotte *could* be wrong.

For forty years Alicia has lived with the same roommate, a little dainty woman—says Charlotte—named Yvonne. A dainty little woman with a soft voice. It was comical to see them together, says Char: Yvonne so little and pretty and Alicia so big and gruff. But they got along fine . . .

Alicia still lives with Yvonne. You think you are getting the picture? You are not getting it. It grows complicated here. It has shadings, shadows.

Alicia protected Ben Gelle, says my friend Philomel Blake from the next block. Philomel is a librarian, and is interested in history.

How—*protected?* I say.

She covered up for him, says Philomel. Ben was an untidy man, mentally. He forgot things. He was rude and arbitrary. Alicia would lie to cover him. And she made excuses for him.

Ben was married, I said.

No, as a matter of fact he wasn't, said Philomel. He was a classical crusty old bachelor. A wretchedly unpleasant man, in most ways.

Sometimes you would catch Alicia looking at that dreadful man, said Philomel, and you would have thought the sun was rising where he stood.

I think she loved him, said Philomel: that's what I think.

Sandra tells me that Alicia wore her black hair, streaked at the last with iron gray, in a short, neat pageboy cut. (That tallies with my picture of her; maybe I really do remember her. . . .)

She was gruff.

She was shy.

In addition to working long hours for low pay in the hardware store, she also wrote out by hand, once a month, the hundreds of bills that Ben sent to charge customers. She did this, Charlotte told me and Sandra one day, for an additional fifteen dollars a month.

Can you imagine? said Charlotte. All those bills? Handwritten? For fifteen dollars?

Why did she do it? Sandra said. For so little?

I don't know, Charlotte said. She just did.

How did she happen to come here? I asked. In the first place?

I don't know, Charlotte said. I guess maybe she just walked in one day, she said: like you did.

There is a potter who has a shop just a few doors down from the corner, on 28th Street. A potter is a person who has moved an infinitesimal distance closer perhaps than the rest of us to stepping off the wheel of time. Choosing to be an artist, or an artisan, choosing that is to submit and bend to the discipline of an art, is perhaps a choice to take this infinitesimal step: to be a little more like God and to be aware of it. I struck up an acquaintance with the potter while I worked at the hardware store: well, I took a class from him, is what happened.

I was not very good at potting. Potting is *terribly, terribly hard.* It looks magically easy when you watch a master, but it is really very hard. I cannot take that particular step in that particular way. Perhaps however working in a hardware store is much the same sort of thing. Perhaps I can make it from where I am.

And in any case, I am going to be an artist of some kind soon. The plan is that I will leave my job at Gelle's so that I can go to art school in March. This is a choice I should have made thirty years ago, but you know how these things go.

One day I was in the pottery shop. I asked him about Alicia.

Alicia? he said.

Big woman, I said. Mannish. Black hair in a pageboy. Overalls.

Sam, he said.

She wasn't mannish, he said. She was very feminine. She didn't wear overalls. She wore brown pants and a brown man's shirt.

But those clothes didn't express *her,* he said. It was just a practical choice.

Really, I said. No overalls.

I never saw her in overalls, he said.

So he and I sat down together in the pottery studio, and he told me about Alicia. He said that where the paint shaker is located now in the hardware store was Alicia's cubby hole years ago. It was a sort of cave built out from the wall that now divides the store proper from the repair area. In this cave (the potter said) Alicia sat and did the books and the billing.

She had her own bookkeeping system, said the potter: I helped Ron Acheson clean the cubby hole out after he took over the store, and we found boxes and boxes piled up there containing cards and names. But they made no sense at all. We couldn't figure out what the system was . . .

It was one of those systems (he said) that depend entirely on the particular people doing it. Alicia and Ben could make it work . . . nobody else could make it work . . .

The potter also told me that the ceiling above Alicia's cubbyhole was dropped, and that there was a space between it and the real ceiling.

Ben had a mattress up there, the potter said. A ladder led up to it. Ben would sleep up there sometimes.

The potter was quiet for a while. I thought he was finished. I thanked him for his information and got up to go.

But he stopped me.

Listen, he said. Wait. There's more.

What I *felt,* he said.

He had a hard time with it. Words are not a potter's proper tools. But finally: She was part of the store, he said. She was the heart of it. That was all there was to say about her. That's *all* she was, after a while.

Are you going to go in on a Saturday and see her? said my friend Philomel.

Oh, no: I said. God. No.

I was astonished. The idea had never occurred to me.

No I couldn't do that, I said.

I suppose not, she said. I suppose it's a story in process of happening, for you. I suppose you can't change the story.

That's it, I said, amazed: that's exactly right. *I can't change the story.*

VIII

Charlotte had for a while some idea that I would be the one to replace her.

Replace you! I said when she first mentioned it: In the first place no one can, and in the second place where are you going? Some day, said Charlotte. I mean someday, not now. I can't stay here forever, she said.

All right, I said. Someday. Ok. That's reasonable. But *me?*

But the idea took hold in my mind. When I thought about it, you know, I was really honored, and touched. That Charlotte, who was so good at it, thought I could do her job: I think I never had a greater compliment. And for a while I thought: Yes, well, why not? I can do it. It would be a good thing to do. I built a fantasy about it: Alicia to Charlotte to me. A chain. A connection.

One of the things I learned to do at the hardware store was to putty new glass into window frames. I also learned to cut glass, but that is no great trick. Window puttying, however, is a special art.

First you must burn and scrape away the old putty, and knock out the old glass. You must be very certain that the surface that is to receive the new glass is scraped clean enough, because even a tiny lump of old putty remaining, even one glazier's point left sticking into the frame, can crack the new glass right across in the blinking of an eye.

You fit the new glass into the window, a bit loose is best. Then you get the glazing gun and with it you shoot glazier's points into the wood frame all around the square to hold the glass in.

Then you put in the putty. Everyone does it a little differently, but the point is always the same: the point is to put in enough putty to hold the glass securely, and to slant the putty at exactly the right angle so that it does not show through the glass on the other side. Charlotte uses a big ball of putty; with two or three deft movements beginning at a corner of the glass away from her and flashing the putty knife toward herself, she lays down enough putty to do one edge of the window. Then she begins again at the corner away from her, cutting the corner into a perfectly slanted and mitered angle, and she brings the knife toward her. In one cut she removes all the excess putty from the strip, and she adds that putty to the ball in her hand. Then she moves the knife lightly over the surface of the putty in a delicate sweep away from her. That final movement makes the line of putty absolutely perfect and smooth. Done wrong, or with anything less than an acutely sensitive touch, that final cut can wreck the whole job. The other fixers in the store—Loren who was in the hospital, Mac, and Garner—didn't try it; they were satisfied without that final perfection. Charlotte does it always. Garner is admiring and jealous. Charlotte is the master, he says. Charlotte is the old damn master. Watch Charlotte, he says.

Charlotte can do the whole operation, start to finish, in about five minutes per window pane. It looks completely effortless when she does it. The first window I did took me over an hour.

God, I feel like such a klutz, I said.

You're doing really well, said Charlotte.

You're kidding, I said.

No, really, said Charlotte. You're really doing it well.

I wasn't always as fast as I am now, she said. I was real slow for at least a year when I started.

Sandra came in. Charlotte told her that I was learning to putty windows faster than anybody else she'd ever taught.

Sandra looked at me. My word, she said. In her cool, cool voice. You must be good. Charlotte hasn't even taught *me* to do windows yet, and here you are doing windows and you've only been here a couple of weeks.

I wonder if that is when she began to dislike me: Sandra. Maybe that is when. And maybe that is why.

I loved working in the hardware store. I loved waiting on customers, and doing windows, cutting keys, helping Charlotte fix things. I enjoyed marking the items that came into the store packed in huge boxes every Tuesday, and I enjoyed shelving them and marking them off on invoice sheets.

It was all absolutely new to me. And so hard for me, my god; so different from the—mainly—desk job I had before. At first I didn't know whether I could do it. I would get so tired. I would go home at noon for my lunch and I would do exercises on the living room floor, because my back hurt so much from all the lifting and bending. At the end of the day I would walk home, my mind with no thought in it but anticipation of a hot bath to soak my muscles; and I would sink into that bath as into the arms of a wonderful lover and there would be no thought in my mind but singing for the feeling of warmth and rest.

I slept well; like a rock; listen, it was the first time in my *life* that I slept well that I can remember. And gradually my back got stronger, gradually I felt altogether stronger and healthier.

Listen: I thanked God for every day. I believe I was happy.

So I began to think: maybe I can do this for the rest of my life. Maybe I will not go to art school after all, maybe I will stay here at the hardware store. It was a fantasy, a pipe dream. I played with it in my mind. I saw myself—Charlotte gone, retired, senile, dead?—holding the tide of progress and order back a little, a little, practicing Charlotte's ways, working the cash register wrong, puttying windows right, stocking shelves whimsically (so no one could find things but me, and they would say about me what they say about Charlotte now: Isn't she wonderful? Isn't Joan wonderful? She knows where *everything* is, she can do *everything* . . .) cutting keys, cutting window shades (the last of the all-time great shade-cutters . . .), fixing toasters for old ladies, charging them nothing or maybe fifty cents, screening baby cribs, for: well: forever. And for love. I liked that dream. It could have worked. Yes. It could have.

One day I said to Sandra:

Sandra, I am at the point where I have to make a decision about going to art school in March. I have been thinking that I might not go. I love it here. I love working here. So I need to know from you whether you think I am doing all right: whether it makes sense for me to want to stay here.

I've been meaning to talk to you about that, she said.

Then she said that she was not happy with me, I did not please her. She said for example that I was not sufficiently aggressive with the customers who came into the store.

God. I was astonished. I was hurt also, but mostly I was astonished. Aggressive. No. I wasn't. It was true.

The thing is, Sandra (I guess, I assume) believes that the purpose of the hardware store is to sell things. I don't know what the purpose of the hardware store is, but I feel certain that it is something else.

What could I do? Sandra is the owner of the store. I registered for art school.

I felt this—something, unnameable, maybe just pique—too deep in myself to talk to Charlotte about it right away. But in a few days I did talk to her.

She said *what!* said Charlotte.

That I was not aggressive enough with the customers, I repeated.

Charlotte's face got suddenly stiff, frozen in a calm mask.

One person she fired because he was *too* aggressive, she said.

Does she think I can stay forever? said Charlotte. I have to leave sometime. *I can't stay . . .*

Listen, Char, I said: Do you remember that time you said I might be able to take your place?

Someone has to. Someday. Said Charlotte. Someone has to.

Her voice was tight. It seemed to me that she was very angry.

I just want you to know that I was proud that you thought I could do it, I said. I just want you to know that, Char.

But I couldn't have done it anyway, Char, I said. I am not strong enough, I am not fast enough.

Yes, well, said Charlotte. And if you have a talent for art, you should go to art school, she said. It's wrong to waste a talent.

Yes, I think I should go to school, I said. But I *would* have stayed here, I said. I *wanted* to stay, I said. I think you should know that, I want you to know that I would have stayed.

Would I really? I don't know. I thought I would have, for a while, but I guess I probably wouldn't have. I am pretty sure I wouldn't have stayed. Not really.

The mistake you make, said Charlotte (later) is in thinking that I am the boss. I am not the boss, she said.

Sandra is the boss.

Yes, well: I said. I am not sorry. I do see you as the boss. *And I am right:* you *are* the boss.

You have to play the game, said Char.

I won't play the game, I said. I've played the goddamn game all my life and I won't play anymore.

I guess you're better off going to art school, Charlotte said.

The Game, folks: in a *hardware store.* In *that* hardware store. God. I was *so shocked.* You know, something about that really got to me; really gets to me.

Well. I *will* go to art school. Will there be a game there too? Maybe. Maybe not. Live in hope. Miracles do happen. God intervenes. Sticks In His Oar, so to speak.

Well, I am laughing. I mean, it's so awful, it's funny. Isn't it? Everywhere you go you find the world.

IX

I was at the hardware store for a total of five months. I saved stamps for Alicia over that entire period of time, except for the first two weeks. The first thing I did every morning at 11 a.m. when I came in was to sort the mail into the kind I could deal with and the kind that Sandra had to see.

The kind that Sandra had to see went into a particular compartment in a drawer.

The kind I could deal with were the envelopes containing checks to pay bills and copies of the bills. I would slit the envelope, carefully so as not to hurt the stamp or the postmark, I mean who knew what order would come next, with a paper knife that Sandra kept for the purpose.

Before I found the paper knife I was opening the envelopes with my hands and I was really wrecking the postmarks and sometimes I would tear a stamp. Finding the paper knife made it all much easier. Every time I picked up the paper knife I felt a little happiness, a little appreciation for it. Even a flicker of gratitude to Sandra. Can you believe that? I am telling you the truth.

The stamps were unremarkable. They were all first class stamps, all the various designs of the first class stamp. There were for example the American Flag stamps. There were the Ralph Bunche stamps—well, as a liberal I hate to admit it, but facts are facts, the Ralph Bunche stamps were boring. Beige and brown. And, once you had a Ralph Bunche stamp, I mean, you had one. More were superfluous.

Ditto the Oliver Wendell Holmes stamps. The Oliver Wendell Holmes stamps had a green line drawing of OWH on a beige background. Nice; but dull.

Then there were the Christmas stamps: the teddy bear on the sled and the Madonna. Separate, I mean. On two separate stamps. Not together.

There was a stamp with a bicycle on it. There were a whole

lot of flower stamps—different flowers on different stamps. Many of each kind of flower.

I saved them all. I really got into it. I really enjoyed this part of my job. Fifteen or twenty minutes every morning saving stamps—carefully, carefully—for Alicia. And thinking about Alicia. I began to know Alicia, it seemed to me that I did. There was something piquant to me, even tragic, in the idea of this queer relationship in which I knew Alicia, and served her, and she did not know me.

I wondered and mused and puzzled: well, when you do a simple-minded thing like saving envelopes with stamps on them, your mind is set free, it can think anything, ask any question. Why did Alicia want these stamps? They were all the same. Nobody could have that many nephews. No nephew would want all those stamps.

As I cut and sorted the envelopes, and saved them in the brown paper bag and concentrated on them, answers began to come to me. Ideas began to come to me.

One idea was that she didn't want the stamps: that she only wanted to come and get the stamps. She was old now, and lonely and sick—I imagined this, I spun out this story for myself—and Yvonne was younger and healthy and still working—Alicia was lonely (on Saturdays? why not? certainly it's possible) when Yvonne was away working. And Alicia had an identity at the hardware store, she came back to visit the scene of that identity, and to be at least on the spot, floor, ground, changed as it was, where she had known (or found, or created) a piece of her self. I knew this Alicia very well—I understood her, I had feeling for her, warmth, sympathy. I knew her.

Another idea that came was that the strokes had softened her brain or something and the stamps were for her. Little colored pieces of serrated paper; I saw her playing with them; I saw her as a big overalled manly child, sorting the Ralph Bunches into one pile, the teddy bears into another. Exulting over the delicate green of the Oliver Wendell Holmeses. Soft in the head—oh, I loved this Alicia. She was happy, this Alicia, this huge child. Brain-damaged baby of the universe: Alicia. I knew her.

One thing that caught my attention in the process of saving the stamps was that sometimes a stamp was not cancelled. This stamp could be used again. The first couple of times I noticed one of these, I didn't pay much attention. The next two, I took for myself; I thought, why not? They are still useful, I might as well have them. God knows they don't pay me much here. This is a bonus. I slipped the envelopes with the uncancelled stamps into the pocket of my red A-1 Hardware smock, and took them home.

Then another Alicia came into my imagination. This one was unspeakably poor, and invented all sorts of desperate stratagems to get hold of money now that she could no longer work. She would have just Social Security; there wouldn't be a pension plan. Not at the hardware store. And the Social Security amount would be low, because it would be based on her wages at the hardware store, and her wages would have been low.

This Alicia saved bottles to turn in at Mellison's. Saved coupons. Collected stamps from Gelle's *to get the uncancelled stamps.* Well, god, was it out of the question? Every day I read in the papers about old people stealing food from garbage cans; this is true, this is really happening. And—from another angle—obviously I felt poor enough to want those stamps, could not Alicia have felt that poor too? *Been* that poor? I was ashamed. The next day I brought the envelopes with the uncancelled stamps back to the hardware store in the pocket of my red smock and I put them into the brown paper bag with the other envelopes.

I put them together on top of the pile. Every day after that I moved all the envelopes with uncancelled stamps to the top of the pile. For them to be all together was, I felt, unmistakably nonaccidental. This was a message which Alicia would receive: Alicia, I understand. Alicia, I have broken your code: I know you.

X

Alicia and the stamps became in a way an obsession for me. I talked about her with a lot of people. One of these people was Philomel from the next block.

Philomel said: I have some Greek stamps from when I went to Greece last summer. Uncancelled. Do you want them for Alicia? I would think Alicia would like them.

I said: Oh, *yes*. That would be great. That would be wonderful.

She said: I think I may have some from London too, and maybe Paris.

Oh, *London. Paris.* I said. They'd be fine. But *Greece!* Greece is wonderful! Alicia will *love* them. I know she will. I said.

So I got from Philomel the stamps from London and Paris and Greece. The London and Paris ones were cancelled and stuck on envelopes—letters which Philomel had sent home to her mother, who lives with her. But the stamps from Greece, six of them, were still together, had not been torn apart, the serrated edges were still intact between them, and there was glue on the backs. And they were beautiful: on each of them there was a circle of Greek dancers in costumes. The colors of the stamps, rose red and blue green, black, yellow, were vivid and primitive, childlike. Compared to Ralph Bunche and OWH they were, well, marvelous, sensational.

I put them into the bag with the other stamps on a Friday, just before I left to go home. I hoped—no, I believed—that Alicia would understand that they were another message from me. Not me, named and known; but me anonymous; a message from someone. Someone interested; someone who in a way cared. I mean, surely uncancelled Greek stamps were unusual enough to be seen as a message. And no one at the hardware store went to Greece on their vacations; people at the hardware store went to Florida.

On the following Monday, the bag of envelopes and stamps was gone. Yes, they told me when I asked, Alicia had been in on Saturday to get the stamps.

So. The message had been sent. The message was now where it belonged. I was content for a while. I went on saving stamps and envelopes in a brown paper bag. Why not? Was it illegal? *Not yet. Sometime soon, folks, but not yet.*

That year we had a terrible winter. In the middle of January on a Wednesday, without any warning at all—I mean, they said three to four inches of snow on the weather forecasts for god's sakes—we had a snowfall of seventeen inches. It was the most snow at any one time that anyone could remember. The buses stopped running—no one could remember when that had happened before either. No one got to work except us at the hardware store of course; we got there because we live right on the block. I struggled through half a block of ice and snow, slipping and sliding, to the store at eleven o'clock and—as always— found Charlotte there ahead of me.

Hi, she said. Isn't this something?

Oh yeah, I said. Something.

It's going to be a busy day, she said.

And it was. We sold every shovel we had in stock. We sold every bag of sand and salt. Every kerosene lantern—the power lines were down some places. Every gallon of gasoline.

Isn't this *something?* everybody said. Isn't this unbelievable? This isn't normal . . .

And then, two days later, on a Friday, it snowed nineteen inches more.

I *mean.* Even for Minnesota, this was bad. We were beginning to think that it signaled the end of the world or something.

Even the media got into it. They did stories speculating on whether we (humankind) have disturbed the balance of things with nuclear testing, etc., and saying that maybe the polar ice caps were melting and shifting, maybe we had created a situation in which a new ice age was upon us.

Nobody in the media went so far as to say that God might be doing it to us on purpose. It occurred to *me* that God might be doing it: as a sort of message, you know, a kind of Shape Up, I've Got You By The Balls statement. From an outraged, or even just neglected, deity.

One Monday after those two storms, I saw that the brown paper bag was still there.

Alicia hasn't been here for a while, I said to Sandra.

Mm, said Sandra.

Charlotte! she called. Have you heard anything from Alicia?

No, Charlotte said: I think the last time she was in must have been the time she bought the Dustbuster.

Charlotte came from behind the cash register and plucked down a slip of paper taped to the wall in back of us.

It was before Christmas, she said: see?

The slip was dated December 21. There was a purchase listed on it: One Dustbuster, $34.95. And her name: Alicia Samson.

That's a big purchase, said Sandra. We'll have to keep an eye on that.

I wish she'd charge on a regular account, like other people, said Sandra.

I know she hasn't come in since then, said Charlotte, because she always settles up anything she owes, whatever it is, large or small, the next time she comes in. She always does that. It's her way. Said Charlotte.

The brown paper bag got so full that I had to start another one.

There the two bags lay then, on the shelf by the cash register, side by side.

The second brown paper bag began to fill up.

Still no Alicia.

This is strange, said Charlotte.

I wonder if something has happened to her, I said. Maybe something has happened to her.

It could just be the bad weather, said Char. It would be hard for her to get here.

Where does she live, I said.

Up on Portland, said Char. About 34th, I think.

My word, I said. That's a long way from here. Has she always lived there?

Yes, always, said Char. Since I knew her.

How in the world did she get *here?* I said. I mean working here?

I don't know how Ben found her, Char said. I don't know how she found Ben.

I remembered then that I had asked this before. The answer was still the same: I don't know.

One day Charlotte said: Alicia could be sick. This long time— this is real unusual, this is not her way.

Maybe she had another stroke, I said. My god, we don't know, she could be dead. I said.

Well, said Char. We could call. She can't call *us,* you know, she can't talk.

Yes, I said. Why don't you call? Here, I'll look up the number. How do you spell her last name?

She's not listed, said Char. You have to look under Yvonne's name: Yvonne Brown.

I looked up the number. There it was: Yvonne Brown. Thirty-sixth and Portland. I wrote the name and the number down on the cover of the phone book.

Um—I am writing the number on the cover of the phone book, Char, I said.

But Charlotte was busy then, waiting on a customer who had just come in.

I overheard a conversation between Charlotte and Sandra the next day.

Joan looked up Yvonne's number, Char said to Sandra. But she didn't call it.

Oh. Why not, said Sandra.

I suppose she thought she didn't know Alicia, Charlotte said. I suppose she thought one of us should do it.

Well. Said Sandra.

XI

My last day at the hardware store has arrived. Friday. Three weeks from Monday I will start going to school. Art school at last; I have been a social worker almost forever and now I am going to art school. Something in me is happy, can hardly believe. Something else is scared. Sad? Maybe sad too.

I want to leave a message—a final message—for Alicia. I want to put it in the brown paper bag with the stamps. Before I leave for work in the morning, I take a three by five card and write: Hi, Alicia. I'm the person who has saved stamps for you since last September. I want you to know that I've enjoyed doing this. I feel that I know you. I feel a connection between us.

I tear the card up. I try again. A new three by five card. *Alicia:* I write at the top of the card.

I stop. My pen stops. There is nothing to say. There is a message all right, but there is no way to say it. I mean, the message is too strange, whatever it is: Alicia, I love you? Is that it? That is not it.

There is no way. Finally I give up. I tear up the second card.
The balance of . . . things . . . seems very delicate to me. *I do not want to disturb the very delicate balance of things.*

I go in to work. On my last day. Charlotte says, I will miss you.
I know that this is a large, an important statement for Charlotte
to make. I feel grateful. Thanks, Char, I say. I'll come back. I'll
let you know how I'm doing.

Maybe I will. Maybe I won't. I am not a great one for coming
back.

I called Alicia, Char says.

Why, my heart nearly stops; my breath stops for a second.
Continues. In-out. Honestly; this is true. Things can take you in
this odd way.

You *did!* I say. But quietly.

Yes, says Char. She won't look at me, Char won't; she stoops
down by a shelf full of light bulbs. She takes a light bulb out.
She dusts it quickly, puts it back. Takes out another.

Alicia answered the phone herself, Charlotte says. If I hadn't
known about her, I would have hung up, she took so long to say
anything, and then what she said was only a sort of noise . . .

But that's wonderful, that you called her, Charlotte: I say.

I told her we were concerned about her, Char says. Charlotte's
voice is shaking a little. Charlotte is crying. Almost. I think so.

It took her such a long time: says Charlotte. It was like she
gathered together all her strength and got behind it and pushed
the one word out . . .

What, Char? I say. What did Alicia say?

She said *Yes,* says Char. Alicia said *Yes.*

Kneeling on the floor of the h.w.s., Charlotte dusts another
light bulb. Puts it back on the shelf where it belongs.

Later. A little. I look around and find an empty box left over from Tuesday when the order came in, and I put into the box the odd accumulation of things that are mine and that still connect me to the hardware store. My calculator, that I brought in one day to help me when I couldn't make the cash register work right. A can of "Lock-Open" that Char said I could have for nothing, it was so old. Some brass screws that almost got swept out with the floor dust one day and that I kept because I figured they were rightfully mine since I had rescued them. Brass screws are better than any other kind and they are pretty expensive. My metal tape measure for measuring glass. You have to measure glass with a metal tape because cloth and plastic tape will stretch just a little and you have to be exactly accurate with glass measurement. Etc. Etc.

And then, when that is done, I settle down to work out my last few hours in the store. And after those few hours I will leave, I will go back into my real life.

Soon I will walk out of the door.

Bye, Char, I will say.

Bye, Char will say.

Will we embrace? Char and I? Who knows? We might—we could do.

I can't hear it—of course not, it's too far away—but I can imagine that down the street the potter's wheel is turning . . . turning.

And all the connections are in place.

All the messages that need to be sent are sent.

Things rest: poised tenderly upon an infinitesimal and unseen balancing point, for today, things rest. Everything is still ok, today.

THE FALL OF A SPARROW

You know that piece in the Bible about God noticing the fall of a sparrow? That stays with me, that idea. That makes me feel—well—not entirely alone out here. You know? I feel noticed. I feel paid attention to.

Not that I am alone, you understand. I have friends; and a part time job; I have family here in Minneapolis: my brother's family, with nephews and nieces. I have my mother in a nursing home over in Northeast to visit one day a week. I have correspondents: my daughter in London, and former teachers of mine around the country, for example; my ex-. (Certainly. Why not?)

I have my house and my plants.

I am fortunate. Very.

But I mean the other aloneness, the kind everyone has. What they call cosmic. The aloneness of each one inside his own head, his own body. Or hers. You know. I don't have to tell you.

I mentioned my plants.

My plants take time every day. I don't have as many of them as I used to, I used to have forty or fifty of them, I tried to count them one day and I kept losing track, I couldn't count them, that's how many I had. Now I have only a few, maybe ten; but they are all special. I expect they will increase over time to forty or fifty again, and maybe this time I will do better, maybe this time I will pay enough attention so that I will know how many there are and treat each one as it deserves.

Take the areca palm, for example. I've had it now for a little more than two years. It is older than that, though. Before it belonged to me, it belonged to Regina, who lived in my house for about a year while I lived in an apartment. Regina uses plants like a lot of people do, for house decor, well I do that too, of course I do, I mean if a plant is *there,* it's *decor,* right? Of course.

But the thing is, Regina has to get rid of plants when they don't look good any more. You could tell that she had tried with the areca: a lot of its tall spears had been cut back and some new little green spears were coming in at the bottom. But I guess it wasn't happening fast enough or something to suit her. I guess she needed it to be beautiful right away; you do when it's decor, obviously. So when she bought her own house and moved out of mine two years ago—two and a half—she didn't take it with her. She left it on my front porch.

Well. I thought she had just forgotten it, you know. So I took care of it for her. I had a new tenant then, a man named Arthur, a photographer, that I had rented one of my upstairs bedrooms to. The plan was that we were going to share the house, Arthur and I.

Arthur told me that the areca palm didn't like a lot of water.

Are you a plant person, Arthur? I asked him.

Well, he said. And shrugged.

Arthur did not ever reveal much about himself.

But all I really needed from him at that time was that piece about the water. Information, knowledge, comes when you need it. Have you noticed that? I notice it all the time. Why, except for Arthur, I might have killed that poor areca, overwatering it, more plants die from overwatering than from any other cause, are you aware of that? Honestly. Overwatering, you could definitely say, is the leading cause of plant death. Worldwide.

Why, my mother, back in the days before she went into the nursing home, when she was staying at my house to take care of the plants when I was away—in Atlanta, I go to Atlanta a lot, my former college freshman English teacher, Elinor, who is now my dear friend, lives in Atlanta—anyway, my mother actually *killed a philodendron* by overwatering it.

And anyone who can kill a philodendron by any means whatsoever is a really gifted killer.

My mother kills plants, but she managed to bring me up without killing me. And my two brothers, the one here and the one who designs airplane engines in Connecticut; they survived her care. So you couldn't call my mother's life a total loss.

But. Back to my story. I guess you are probably wondering how I can call this a story, since nothing is happening. In a story something has to happen. Right? But the thing is, something *is* happening in my story; you just aren't counting it, you aren't noticing, you aren't paying close enough attention. Something is happening here.

Anyway, I called Regina after a week or so, when I had watered the areca maybe once, after I found out from Arthur that it didn't need a lot of water.

Regina, I said. Over the telephone. Is that you, Regina?

It's me, she said.

You don't sound like yourself, I said: over the telephone. Are you sure it's you?

Goddamn, she said. Of course I'm sure it's me.

Well: I said: I have never had occasion before to talk to you in a non-landlord/tenant connection.

Why are you calling now? she asked. This *is* Joan, isn't it?
Yes, I said.
Who else? said Regina. She laughed. I guess she thinks I'm
kind of goofy. Well, a lot of people do. Think so. But she likes
me anyway. A lot of people do: like me.
Who else could I have a conversation like this with? Regina
said. Giggled.
Normally, Regina does not giggle. She laughs gently, in a way
that I personally find kind of patronizing. Regina has a lot of
dignity, and is an important person: a director of social service
in a big agency in Minneapolis.
You left a couple of things here, Regina, I said. You left an
electric wok. And your big areca palm is on the front porch.
Ok, she said. I'll come over tomorrow. Or the next day.
Thanks. She said.
And the next day, when I came back from my job—I work in
people's houses, taking care of old people—the wok was gone,
and the areca palm was sitting out in the alley next to the
garbage cans.

I didn't take it in right away, you know. I mean, a plant that
Regina doesn't want: I thought: what do I want with such a plant?
But. It got to me. It was like it was talking to me without say-
ing a word.
Help me. Help me. It was saying. *I'm alive. I'll grow for you.
Honest. I promise. I'm something. I'm not nothing.*
What can you lose? it would say. Every damn time I came
home it would be yelling at me.
Help me, help me. Ohhh. Take care of me. Pay attention.
Finally I gave in. I picked it up—and with my bad back that
was a big deal all by itself, the pot was at least ten inches across,
maybe twelve, big, *heavy*—I got my arms around the pot and
carried it into my house and put it on the floor in the corner of

the dining room in an east window.

There, I said: now grow.

It was such a tatty-looking thing. I'm telling you. It was piti-ful. Maybe five feet tall—one tall spire ending in a single fan leaf—and straggly, with a few new spears just starting at the base, maybe a foot or a foot and a half high. I mean, at the best of times an areca is not, to my way of thinking, a beautiful plant; it's always kind of thin-looking; even a good areca; and this was a long way from a good areca.

I'll give you a chance, plant, I said. I really wasn't very nice to it. Calling it "plant" that way. Just barely putting up with it, you understand.

I see you took the plant in, said Arthur when he got home that evening.

Yup, I said.

What else could I do? I said.

I really felt kind of cross about it. What am I, a hospital? The damn thing kept yelling at me. I said.

Mm, said Arthur.

Arthur was kind of noncommittal all the time. He never said much; ever. I mean, *Mm* is as close to nothing as you can get. It seems to me.

Well, over the months—years now, going on three—the areca grew marvelously. My theory is that the poor thing was so grate-ful to me for being brought back from the garbage that way that it made up its mind to grow its little heart out.

I contributed something, of course. Water. (Only a very little, comparatively speaking. Compared for example to a hibiscus, which needs lots.) That east window. New earth now and then; I never actually repotted it, it was just too big, but I did what they call "topping": that is taking the old dirt off the top with a spoon or something—a trowel is too sharp, you might damage the roots—and then replacing the old dirt with new dirt around the roots.

Also, I talked to it. Well, I talk to all of them.

You can do it, dear, I would say. (I got over calling it "plant" quite soon; it became "dear" like all the others. My plants don't have names. Some people's do. Guinevere. Bridget. Thomas. Or like that. But not mine, not yet anyway. It just doesn't take me that way. Yet.)

You need a new leaf just here, I would say. That would fill up this hole. Can you do it? Try, dear; I absolutely believe you can.

Anyway, the areca grew and grew. It is taller than I am now. It has filled in wonderfully at the bottom.

My friend Evalyn—who is a florist, sometimes I work in Evalyn's shop—asked me one day to make a design for the cover of her new advertising brochure: Just something very simple, she said, just a line drawing of a big plant that would be suitable for an office.

I made several drawings for Evalyn: one of a fig—ficus, that is—fiddle-leaf. A very tall dracaena variety: a corn plant. And a drawing of the areca against a background of a Levelor window shade: very office-ish, I thought.

Well—this is the one, Evalyn said, meaning the drawing of the areca. This is beautiful. This is perfect.

Then she looked at the areca itself, that I had made the drawing from. Why, she said, that's a perfect plant. Absolutely perfect. Every stalk just where it ought to be. Every leaf. Where in the world did you get that areca?

Oh—well: I said. Hm.

I can keep my mouth shut sometimes. I can be as clammish as Arthur. I really couldn't say: from the garbage: could I?

Ho-ho. You hear that, dear? You are perfect. Perfect. A florist says so.

Eat your heart out, Regina.

Arthur did not stay long—maybe three months. The thing was, he couldn't get a job. Well, he hadn't any practical experience, you know; he had just finished a photography course somewhere in Illinois, and he hadn't yet got a job. Well, he had a *little* job that didn't pay much working as a drudge for another photographer; but he couldn't live on what he made at that job. He was older, you see; maybe forty years old. The older you get, the more things you realize you have to have: until you get really old, that is. A car. A phone machine. When you are twenty you can live on nothing, on minimum wage; at forty you need more.

At forty you are also paying child support; Arthur was paying child support for a son somewhere in Minneapolis. He didn't say a lot about it. But I did know that much.

Arthur never gave up. I had to admire that about him. Every day he worked, and every night he sent out letters and resumes. And messages would be left on our answering machine. Sometimes the messages would grant him an interview.

But, you know, the thing is, he wasn't a very good photographer.

From what I saw.

In my opinion.

My sister-in-law gave me a plant a few months ago. Doris, her name is. My sister-in-law's name, I mean; like I said, I haven't gotten to naming plants yet.

Do you want my big arrowhead plant? Doris said.

Well—sure, I said: Ok. But why?

Well, she said. I'm sick of it. I can't get it to do anything. I guess I haven't got the right light, or something.

Well. Ok. I said.

What am I, a hospital?

Well, the poor thing when it came was really sad: straggly, spindly, yellow. Dying leaves all over it. There were three plants, and they were in a big clay pot.

Maybe the pot is too big, I said to my friend the florist. I don't think so, she said: there are three plants there, it could fill out after a while.

So. Maybe overwatering. I let it dry out pretty much and then I watered it again, but not too much. I cut off all the dying leaves. I threw them in the garbage, but I did it quite gently, and I told them they were going home. Which they are, you know; to earth; after a while.

Then I put the pot in my east window, on a little table next to the areca. I had to move a couple of African violets and a begonia to free up the space, but I explained to them why it was necessary, and that it was only temporary, for the recovery period. I moved them into a kitchen window, and they seem ok with it, in fact the African violets love it, they are blooming like crazy, I may leave them there.

Well, the arrowhead plant—sagittaria, as you perhaps know if you are a plant person—is thriving. You should see it: my friend the florist was right, it has filled the whole big pot. It is getting new leaves all the time. Right now there are three new ones coming in.

I check on the new leaves every day.

How are you doing, honey? I say. Or sweetheart. To each leaf, because in a way they *are* separate, you know. Not just pieces of a big plant.

There was one leaf at the beginning that simply refused to open up, no matter how encouraging I was. A couple of weeks went by and that leaf just stayed furled, it wouldn't open.

Well, I figured it out, of course. One does. The thing is, that leaf had a blemish, a dried up spot, maybe some too-strong fertilizer had got on it and burned it or something. Something had happened to it. Anyway, it was, you know, embarrassed. I mean, it knew it was going to have a hole in it when it opened, so it just stayed furled, so as not to display that hole. The poor thing was ashamed. Can you believe it?

Dear, I said to it. When I figured it out. You can open, dear; we have room for all kinds here. It's ok to have a hole. There's a space here that's never going to be filled if you don't fill it. Honestly, dear. I wouldn't lie to you.

(I would, you know: lie: but it would be meant well. I would lie for the plant's own good.)

Anyway, the leaf did open, it is open now, it is filling the space very well. And it seems quite happy.

My brother was over the other day.

Is that Doris's plant? he said.

Well. I said. It used to be; mine now.

But that's that dead old plant?

Yup. I said.

How do you do it? he said.

Well, I said: I just, you know, take care of them. Pay attention to them.

I suppose you talk to them. He laughed.

Well, sure I do, I said; I do talk to them. Of course.

Do you play music for them too? (I believe he thought he was being sarcastic. My brother is a very nice man, I love him dearly, but he'd never be a plant person. Not as he is now. He could, however, change, I guess. There's hope for any of us. I guess.)

Rock 'n' roll?

Well, no. I said. Mozart. Actually. If you want to know.

Mozart, he said. He came over and gave me a big hug and kissed my cheek. Laughed. My big sister, he said. Jeez. Tch.

I guess he thinks I'm crazy. Nice, but crazy.

But he didn't grow that plant, did he?

I personally prefer Mozart too. Over all the others; more than any other music. Better for growth too: that incredible spurting dazzling fountain of pure joy and liveliness, that exact delicate celebration.

I used to like rock, but not so much anymore.

Don't get me wrong, I still like it. But I like Mozart better.

II

One day there began to be a lot of messages on the machine for Arthur from relatives: Arthur, this is your sister Karen; call home. 716-5126. This is Ben, call home right away. We'll all be at Karen's, probably, call me there. 716-5126. Arthur, this is Karen again; *please call. Please.* 716-5126.

I heard these messages because now and then there was a message for me, and in order to get that message, I had to listen to all of Arthur's messages.

Well, it made me nervous, all those urgent messages. When I gave them to him I had them written down. Call Karen. Call Ben. Call home. The written-down messages didn't convey the sound of the voices, which was of course where the real message was.

I thought those voices said: We love you, Arthur. We want you. This is important. Pay attention.

So I would give him the written-down list of calls, but I would also say: They sounded really urgent, Arthur. They sounded like they really wanted you to call.

Oh, he said: yeah. Ok.

But I think he didn't call back, because the calls kept coming.

This went on for—what? days, anyway. Maybe a week.

I'm telling you. It was making me so ungodly nervous.

One day a call comes for Arthur when I am at home to answer it. Hello, I say. Hello, is Arthur Allen there? says this woman's voice. Karen, I'll bet anything. No he isn't, I say; this is his, um, landlady, I say, can I give him a message? I say.

This is his sister Karen, she says. Look, I really hate to do this. But he doesn't answer our calls.

So what else can I do? she says.

Please tell him that his sister Patty died. She says. Please tell him the funeral is on Friday and we want him to come. Tell him we really, really want him.

Uh, I say.

I mean, gosh, I am a stranger, I don't know this person who has died at *all,* and even I feel like I've been kicked.

Will you? she says.

Well. I say. Sure. Of course. I'll tell him. Sure. Of course.

There's another call, from Ben, a little later. Ben, I call him; like I knew him; well, I feel like I do, by now, you know. Know him. I feel like I know the whole family. Tell Arthur we really want him, Ben says. Tell him we'll pay for the ticket home if he's short . . .

Tell him if he wants to talk to us we're at 716-5126. Area code 146.

I think about it all day, how to do this. Should I wait until he's had his supper and settled down a bit? Or should I, like, hit him with it immediately? Wouldn't it seem strange if I waited? Should I, well, tell him to, you know, *sit down* first? That's what they do in books . . .

Well, of course, fussing about it in my mind made no difference at all, because I just blurted it out almost the minute he got home. I was upstairs, and I heard him come in the front door and walk toward the kitchen. I came down the stairs and there he was with his hand on the big iron fry pan, just taking the cover off, I remember that, and I said, Arthur, your family called to tell you that your sister Patty died, they asked me to tell you, I'm so sorry . . .

I put my hand on his on top of the fry pan cover: I'm so sorry,

I said.

Oh. He said.

They want you to come to the funeral, I said. It's on Friday. They left a number. They said they'd pay for a ticket . . .

Ok, he said. He moved his hand away from mine. He lifted the cover off the heavy pan and set it down on the next burner on the stove. He went over to the fridge and got out a casserole, went back to the stove and dumped half of the casserole's contents into the fry pan.

Got to feed the inner man, he said softly. Laughed softly.

See, he said, we all knew she was going to die. This has been going on for years. She was a diabetic.

So it isn't as if this is a surprise. He said.

But thank you for telling me. Said Arthur. Stirred his supper.

But I saw his eyes, you know. They were bright as blood, and full of fear.

Shock. They call it shock, you know. What you do right away when you hear some very bad news. You maybe start to laugh and you say crazy things.

Or go on eating your supper.

It's just shock, they'll say. Plants can have it too.

Anyway, Arthur ate his supper.

I had a plant once that committed suicide. Honestly. Well, I have to admit that I helped it along a little at the end when I saw what was happening. So. Part suicide and part euthanasia. You could say.

What happened was this: I bought that plant (it was a small schefflera; generally a very difficult plant to begin with, I mean, if you don't want neurosis don't get a schefflera!*) anyway, I bought the schefflera in Atlanta a long time ago, seventeen years ago, when I was visiting my friend Elinor, I mentioned her before.

* A regular schefflera, I mean. The Hawaiian schefflera is easy: a very undemanding plant.

You are buying a plant in Atlanta to take to Minneapolis? said Elinor.

Well, it *is* crazy, isn't it? I said.

Kind of, said Elinor. Laughed. She likes me and is more or less on my side no matter how weird I get.

I have *taken* to this plant, I said. And this plant has taken to me. I have to get it.

I said.

Mm, she said. But I knew what her Mm meant: not like Arthur's Mm. So that was ok.

That schefflera was with me for about fifteen years. For most of that time it grew tremendously. It was maybe ten inches tall when I got it, and it grew to be much taller than me. And strong. Healthy. With very large leaves: you know how the schefflera grows, in clusters of leaves coming out from a center, like the ribs of an umbrella: actually, they do call it an umbrella plant. Familiarly.

That plant had a peculiarity, though. It became like my shadow; or my mirror. Whenever I was sad or sick or in any way *down,* that plant drooped, dropped leaves. For example.

When I was ok, it thrived.

It took me years to figure this out, of course, that this was what was happening. I mean, it isn't an obvious deduction, is it? Actually, it's fairly odd. Isn't it?

But it happened over and over again and I finally saw it and I began to use that plant as a sort of psychic thermometer.

Yup, I would say when that plant drooped and dropped leaves. There is something wrong with me. I had better figure out what it is and get happy again. And I would do that, and the schefflera would perk up.

And so it would go.

One day I got a notion. My notion was that I was getting too old to take care of a house, to shovel snow and cut the grass and go running up and down stairs, all like that.

Eventually I decided to rent the house to Regina and move into a big, beautiful modern apartment with my friend Evalyn, the florist.

Listen, that was a *great apartment.* It had a patio with a balcony and a big glass door looking out over the balcony and Lake Calhoun. A huge living room: all white, elegant as hell. Available sauna, whirlpool bath, indoor and outdoor swimming pools. I mean, god, *tennis courts.* And near the lakes; Minneapolis has wonderful in-city lakes. I mean, altogether, an absolutely enviable place to live.

I brought the schefflera with me, of course, I mean I couldn't consider anything else. The other plants I mostly left for Regina, who promised to take care of them. But the schefflera I moved to the new apartment, and I sat with it in the back of Evalyn's floral van the whole way and told it where we were going, etc., etc.

Well, goddamn it. The schefflera hated that apartment. *Hated it.* There it was, in that wonderful big east window with a view of Lake Calhoun, and it became absolutely clear after about six weeks that the damn plant was terribly unhappy.

But I had my notion to contend with: you know, the one about how I was getting too old to take care of a house? And— like a lot of people—I am funny about notions. I am very stubborn about them. The crazier they are, the more I cling to them. Have you seen that too? It takes a *really crazy, silly notion* to produce a big defense: a war, for example. People get very hot over crazy notions. I have never seen the same passion engendered by sane notions: peace; ecology. For example. I mean, have you? There's something about sanity that sort of rules out heat.

I *wanted* life in that apartment to work. It was a dumb idea, but I *wanted* it.

But it didn't work. Of course it didn't. I mean, think about it. Can you see me in an elegant modern white apartment? With tennis courts?

Evalyn, yes. Evalyn did fine. Not me.

There's no point in going into a lot of detail. But the end of it was this: one day I saw that the schefflera was sick to death, was dying. I finally saw that, and I finally gave up on it, and gave up on the whole thing. Goodbye, dear, I said one day, and I broke off all of its draggly drooping brown leaves and cut its stem off down by the pot and made it into a stick, which as a matter of fact I still have.

It cost me a lot to get out of that apartment arrangement and move back into my house—almost two thousand dollars. But except for losing the schefflera it was all worth it. I learned something. I learned to stay where I am and give up notions.

Arthur moved out of my house soon after his sister died; he broke his lease with me and went to Chicago, where he said he'd have a better chance at getting a job as a photographer.

Well. You know what I think; I already told you. But what do I know? Miracles happen. They do.

I am doing fine. My plants are thriving. I am working my way back to forty or fifty of them. The stick that is all that remains of my schefflera rests against the wall near the east window in the dining room where Regina's areca and Doris's arrowhead plant—mine now—still live.

The stick reminds me of my narrow escape. The way I think of it, that schefflera, you know, *died for me?*

I think I would have died in that apartment.

I imagine you think I am crazy. I imagine you think I am a crazy old lady dithering around with ten or twelve plants—heading toward forty or fifty—in a house on Delaware Avenue in South Minneapolis.

But what if you're wrong? Maybe I am something else. Maybe I am the piece of God that knows and takes care of all the separate leaves on Doris's arrowhead plant: mine now. Maybe there's another piece living somewhere down the street that—for example—notices the fall of a sparrow and numbers the hairs on your head.

Maybe there's a piece in Chicago right now talking to Arthur. Renting him a room, maybe. Noticing him.

I guess this sounds screwy. But how do you know? How do you know that the whole thing couldn't be organized that way? I mean, *how do you know?* Fifteen out of twenty plant people, worldwide, will tell you that it *could be.*

THE BOOK OF DREAMS ────────────────

I keep a journal of dreams. Sometimes stories come out of the dreams. I never know when the stories will come, or whether. I know this: that they demand to be written so they can find their endings.

This is the way it works: I do not know how a story will end. I begin with a piece that I have, and I write it down, and sometimes the end comes and is written down too. When that happens, I am delighted and amazed: I read it and marvel—well, and so *this* is the end! I say to myself. So *this* is what was wanted! When that does not happen, it does not matter as much as you might think. So, it was not a story after all, I say to myself: I was mistaken.

Either way, I have done my job. I have found the piece that looked like a story and I have done what I could with it.

Well, but you can see that there is another possibility here: that they are all stories, that there is no piece that is not a story; and that the mistake is in me, that I am not clever enough to find the ending.

A third possibility: that I am simply deluded and there are no stories at all, and no right endings. I am—I have to admit it—never entirely sure: sometimes I read the right, amazing ending over and it has turned into wooden words. Maybe I am—you can see how this might be true—just another nut case. A voice crying in the forest where the witch and the children live forever; well, and if there is no forest? Simply a voice? Crying?

That would be sad, unfortunate, and possibly even pitiful; but hardly amazing and delightful. Not good enough. Not enough to tantalize anyone with: to lure anyone to follow a trail of bread-crumb words through the forest to the—what?—at the center. Well, I didn't tell you, did I? You have to follow me or you'll never know if I can find the ending.

This story was written down in the book of dreams. I found it a few days ago, and I was astonished: what in the world is this, I thought: what in the world was I thinking when I wrote this down? The pieces don't seem to fit together at all this time; there are two pieces written down together in the book, but the connection is lost. And yet I think, you know, that they are just as likely to make a story as any other two pieces; surely you can see that that is the case: either all the stories are stories or else there are no stories? either all the pieces are connected or none of them are?

I do go on, don't I? Well, I am like that. Maybe you will like me and maybe you won't, it doesn't make a difference to me.

But as a matter of fact I think you *will* like me! Unwilling, unwanting, you are caught, thraught, thrall.

Listen, put up with me: I mean, can it hurt you?

Listen. Please like me. Please.

Once, quite a long time ago, I went to a concert given by Pete Seeger. The concert was the first one that he gave in our town after the ban of the black years—*red years? ha-ha*—was lifted.

The concert was very good, and one part of it was wonderful. That part came near the end, when Pete Seeger said he wanted to give us—the audience, me—something; which was given to him, he said, long years past, by Woody Guthrie. It was a song. Woody Guthrie, Pete Seeger said, had "given" it to him with the statement that some day it "might help." And now he would "give" it to us, because some day it "might help."

I remember that I was tense and caught, waiting; I mean, I need all the help I can get, don't you? I am always waiting for the magic thing that might help. Help what? Well, you know; you know the caught, frightened, helpless thing in you, the ghost, the child. *That cries in the forest? Maybe. Maybe that's it. Maybe that's where we're going . . .*

This was the song: you know it: *You got to walk . . . that lonesome valley . . . You got to walk it . . . by yourself . . . Nobody else . . . can walk it with you . . . You got to walk it by yourself . . . You got to walk . . . etc.*

Well, you know that song. That's all there is to it, there is nothing much to it. What kind of a gift is that? How can that help? You just sing—he just sang—those words over and over again. It becomes a chant. It gets louder and louder. It gets faster and faster. It gets sort of happy, sort of jazzy. There is magic in it. After a while it does help. I don't know how this happens.

Try it. You'll see. And listen, it's free. I am giving you this free. It was a gift to me from Pete Seeger. Who had it from Woody Guthrie.

Another time, a friend of mine, Elinor Martin, who was my English teacher many years ago, told me that the secret dream of her life was to be a ballet dancer. This was hilarious, since Elinor is very short, not five feet tall, and round, fat even. We had seen a movie with wonderful dancing in it, "Singin' in the Rain"—the first time it was shown, maybe thirty-five years ago, maybe longer than that—and it was raining when we came out of the theater, and Ellie put up her little yellow umbrella against the rain and then she told me her dream and she began to hum and suddenly she went pirouetting down the street in her yellow umbrella and her yellow raincoat, dancing and singing away from me in the rain, a short, plump teacher of English; and it was strange, but I could see how it might have been. I could see a tall thin Ellie freed for the moment and dancing. Little feet in black rubber boots splashing and dancing through puddles, little hands on short arms making jerky and tentative motions in the rain, little yellow umbrella waving: and inside of it all was this tall thin person made of light. I saw this thin person for just a second. I give this person presents at Christmas sometimes: thin serpentine chains of gold at Christmas to wear on thin white wrists.

Well, and then I got interested in the secret dreams. I have been interested in them for many years now. I sometimes ask people about them. I worked once with a woman named Barbara who was a nurse, and very good at her job. She liked being a nurse. But nursing is hard work. And her job was exceptionally hard. Her patients were blind diabetics in a rehabilitation center. Barbara got very tired, strain showed in her face.

—Barb, I said to her one day, do you have a secret dream of something you'd rather be than a nurse?

—Who wants to know? she said.

—Well, me, I said. I do. I am writing a story about secret dreams and I would like to put your secret dream into my story.

—That's easy, she said then. It wasn't easy, though, apparently; she waffled and hesitated quite a bit before she came out with it.

But she did tell me. What I really want to be, she said, is a lighthouse keeper in a small lighthouse on the Atlantic coast.

Then she thought about it some more. It's never the Pacific, she said, it has to be the Atlantic. And preferably New England. Absolutely preferably Maine. But it's always a lighthouse . . . always me being a lighthouse keeper. Alone. I'm always alone.

Vange, who is a social worker, wants to be a singer; it doesn't matter what kind, opera, folk, pop, it doesn't matter. But she wants to have a marvelous, spectacular voice that people would pay money to hear. Vange is tone-deaf and has a harsh, hoarse voice. For a long time she wouldn't sing at all. Then I convinced her that it was ok to sing; now she sings whenever people are singing in an authorized way, Happy Birthday or Christmas carols or something like that, the Star-Spangled Banner, you know; but she sings softly in a sort of tuneless growl so as not to throw the rest of the singers off.

Orville Norlinger, who is legally blind and has cerebral palsy, as well as a great many other problems, a severe speech impediment for example, was one of the people that I put my question to: what is your secret dream, Orville? I said. What is it you want to be in your deepest heart? He took the question and the answer seriously; well, though, most people did, not just Orville.

—I wuh-wuh-wanted to buh-buh-buh-be a Suh-certified Puh-puh-puh-Public Accuh-cuh-cuh-cuh, he said. Gasped and started over: Accuh-cuh-cuh-cuh.

—Accountant, I said. Ordinarily I let Orville finish his words no matter how long it takes, it seems to me that is only respectful, but this is so bad. And my fault.

—Yuh, yes, he says.

Orville is one of the calmest, sweetest-natured people I know, but apparently the question has touched a sensitive nerve. His face, lined and twisted from the spasms of his ailment, is suddenly clouded as he tells me that when he was a young man in college they told him that to be a CPA was out of the question and so he majored in sociology instead.

—I cuh-could have, he says. They were ruh-ruh-wrong.

—What is your secret dream, Sarah? I say to my dearest

friend. Sarah Richardson and I have been friends since I was seventeen and she was eighteen, and it is a long time since then, but I have never known this about her. She doesn't tell me right away, she hedges and hesitates.

—God, Joan, I've never told anyone about this, she says. It's my deepest, darkest secret . . .

—Tell, I say. And I'll put it in a story.

—Don't laugh, she says. You have to promise.

I promise. What can it be. Theft? Killing? To be the greatest counterfeiter in human history?

—I want to be a professional golfer, she says.

Oh.

And yet. I think of Sarah, middle-aged, anxious, lean, spare, unhappy, released in the arc of a golf club's swing into grace, certainty.

—Ok, I say. Yes, that's good. That's a good secret dream.

—Is it all right? says Sarah.

—Yes, it's all right, I say.

—Is it a good enough secret dream? she says.

—It's good enough, I say.

So then, these are the two parts that were written down together in the dream-notebooks: the song that Pete Seeger gave me that might help, and the secret dreams. And there is an inked-in star by the side of the paragraph in the notebook, in the left-hand margin; the star says: There is a story here. Remember this.

I wanted (in my own secret dream) to be a folk singer with a guitar. Like Pete Seeger, sort of. Perhaps not quite so topical. I wanted to sit cross-legged at the edge of a stage with my long hair flowing down, Joan Baez style, and sing my true heart in a straight line to the people listening. (People *would* listen. Always. I would be adored.)

This is so silly: I can't even sit cross-legged. I broke my hip falling down the stairs when I was two years old, and even in kindergarten I couldn't sit cross-legged.

And I have no musical ability whatsoever.

Actually, I am a social worker. Like Vange. Or I was for a long time. Now I am something else, and in between then and now, I have been many things. An art therapist. A clerk in a hardware store. A student. A floral designer. For example. I have tried many things, searching for the exactly right thing. People tell me that I have courage, but actually it is restlessness. I am a restless woman; I search and I change and I go here and there.

It doesn't matter at all. Is this the loaf at the end of the breadcrumb trail in the heart of the forest: that it doesn't matter at all?

Yes; maybe. Maybe that's it.

All of the secret dreams and their dreamers clasp hands in a long chain, the ballet dancer and the golfer and the singer and the lighthouse keeper and the CPA, and Barb and Ellie and Sarah and Orville and Vange and me and you, and Joan Baez and Pete Seeger and Woody Guthrie, and we dance; and as we dance we sing the song that Pete Seeger gave us (that Woody gave him) and we sing other songs too and sometimes it helps and sometimes it doesn't, and some of the dreams are good enough and others are not, some of the dreams come true and others don't, and listen: it doesn't matter.

This is what it is: there is something else happening besides my life: another dream, more secret still.

COLOPHON

The text of this book was set in Adobe Garamond type with Helvetica display. It was printed on acid-free paper, and smyth sewn for durability and reading comfort.